Made Things

ALSO BY ADRIAN TCHAIKOVSKY

Guns of the Dawn
Dogs of War
Spiderlight
Ironclads
The Expert System's Brother
Cage of Souls
Walking to Aldebaran

THE CHILDREN OF TIME
Children of Time
Children of Ruin

ECHOES OF THE FALL
The Tiger and the Wolf
The Bear and the Serpent
The Hyena and the Hawk

MADE THINGS

ADRIAN TCHAIKOVSKY

A TOM DOHERTY ASSOCIATES BOOK

NEW YORK

MADE THINGS

Cover art by Red Nose Studio
Cover design by Christine Foltzer

Edited by Lee Harris

A Tor.com Book
Published by Tom Doherty Associates
120 Broadway
New York, NY 10271

www.tor.com

Tor® is a registered trademark of
Macmillan Publishing Group, LLC.

ISBN 978-1-250-23298-4 (ebook)
ISBN 978-1-250-23299-1 (trade paperback)

First Edition: November 2019

Thank you to my agent, Simon Kavanagh, and my editor, Lee Harris, for bringing this project to reality, and also to Red Nose, for the two reprobates on the cover

Made Things

1.

COPPELIA ALWAYS GOT TOO into her performances. For an actual puppeteer it would have been a good trait, but for a thief it was terrible. Still, she was doing *Simeon the Garden-Born,* and that was worth doing well. She had just about tuned out her audience, no idea whether there were coins in the hat as she did the bit where Simeon the grown-thing confronts his creators for the first time, the scarecrow figure lifting its leaf-ended arms piteously and the squeaky voice she gave it denying the grim destiny fate had set out for it. When she looked up, there were a couple of Broadcaps in the audience and everyone else was either sidling away or obviously more interested in her getting a kicking than good puppetry.

She knew all three of them. Fountains Parish was her stamping ground and all the local law were familiar faces, though more celebrated in their absence than their almost-within-arm's-reach presence. Belly Keach was a nasty brute if he got his hands on you, but he wasn't exactly a pal for chasing you anywhere or working up a sweat. Beside him was lean, bony Lynx Soriffo—the name he was actually born with and woe betide any street scum trying to give him a new one. He was religious in that particular way that meant he took a sanctimonious pride in the whippings he doled out for petty offences, such as being poor and not running away fast enough. On the other hand, Coppelia knew of an obliging lady who laid stripes on his bony buttocks three times a week and she reckoned that this knowledge served as a shield of sorts against him truly getting into his swing.

The Catchpole in charge of them was Lucas Maulhands, though, and he was another matter entirely, shorter than either of them with knuckles like the studs on a bailiff's club. And clever, and at least a half-mage, just like she was.

He had his arms folded, those strangler's mitts of his half out of sight in the baggy sleeves of his blue robe. The other two had their hats on still, wide navy brims shading their faces from the heat of near-noon, but old Lucas didn't care about the sun on his stubbly scalp, and wasn't sweating, either, some charm of his underclothes doubtless keeping him cool. Which led Coppelia to wonder how she might abstract those items from his person or his nightstand, because if you were a thief in Loretz, then your fingers itched for the magic the place was famous for. Her parents had travelled there from eighty miles distant, looking for the city of magi that would value both their arcane and their artisanal skills.

It hadn't worked out for them. Whether it was working out for Coppelia was a question each day had a new answer for, but she hadn't looked back when she crept out of the orphanage window.

Maulhands had been after her back then—not a Catchpole yet, but a tireless hound in the service of the Convocation—and had never caught her, which meant she was a fishbone lodged in his throat as far as he was concerned. Just her luck to snag one of the few Broadcaps who actually burned with a need to do his duty rather than just take some coin on the side and turn a blind eye. Not that she had the coin right now.

And she was actually a thief, and this performance, through some fairly oblique means, was accessory to larceny. And if he had wanted to just run her in for no reason at all, he'd be within his rights to do that, too, because she was one of the teeming multitudes from the Barrio and that made her fair game this side of the river.

He caught her eye, did Maulhands. He had a face like an old envelope, creased and rectangular, burned manila by the sun. One of those creases was the crook of his narrow mouth; a man willing to stretch his sacred duty by just enough to get one particular guttersnipe into the stocks or to the whipping post. Or perhaps he really was as straight as he made out and just assumed she was about some piece of villainy, in which case he'd be right and it wouldn't help her anyway.

Seeing they weren't going to descend on her and just kick apart the opened-up box she was using as a stage, Coppelia mustered her dignity and went on with the scene. She'd spent all last night kenning the speeches, after all. She might as well make the most of them. She kept her eyes strictly on her little mannikins or the Broadcaps, because her accomplices were out there and, who knew, they might pull something out of the fire. They were a resourceful lot, and Maulhands didn't know about them.

Oh, when he and his sauntered into Redfountain Square, doubtless he looked all around for the pocket-dippers taking advantage of her little show. Perhaps there had even been some, making themselves scarce the moment the authoritarian blue caught the corner of their eye. Nobody who had tipped her the nod, of course, like a good confederate should have done, but Maulhands probably assumed she'd pissed off her mates again. He'd received more than a few choice handfuls of sharp change from her tongue before, mostly hurled over her shoulder in headlong flight. He must guess she was short of close pals in the Barrio.

He wasn't to know she'd made some new friends in the months since their paths had crossed last, and they were there and present in Redfountain, going about a cutpurse's business as best they could, right under everyone's noses.

The last speech done, Coppelia had her puppets solemnly bow before her diminished audience, and most specifically to the three Broadcaps. Lynx looked like the whole business had been lemons on his tongue, and Belly Keach tugged at the high collar of his shirt beneath his robe, where the sweat and the grime were fighting a war that would go on until cold weather ended campaigning season. Lucas Maulhands clapped precisely twice.

"Moppet," he named her. "How about you let my Lynx here relieve you of whatever you're holding that's not yours, and then you can come back to the Blue House and take your stripes."

She gave him a look as guileless as a child's. "Why, Catchpole Lucas, you're never telling me there's a law against puppetry now?"

He examined the knuckles of his big right hand, one of which bore a crescent scar made by her teeth six years before, when he had come closest to snaring her. "Now, don't let's make this difficult—"

"But Catchpole, my business here is merely to entertain, and if these worthies feel my efforts are sufficient, then perhaps generosity may move them to deposit a coin or two as a token of their estimation." She risked a look at the hat. Apparently, generosity was wary of getting its lily-white flesh sunburned today and was staying indoors. "Or if you're referring to that other business you and I once engaged in, Catchpole, I'm seventeen now, too old to be returning to the orphanage."

"Not too old for the workhouses," Lucas said bleakly, and he must have seen and treasured her flinch. Her parents had been in the workhouses, just like any poor immigrants with magical ability. And from the workhouses they had been taken, and that had been that.

"I bind no powers here, nor work any craft. Even my little friends have naught to them but wood and rags." She dangled the Simeon figure on the end of its strings. And Lucas had enough mage in him that he'd know she was telling the truth, if truth's feeble ribbons were something he'd let himself be bound by.

His eyes squeezed almost shut with suspicion. She saw in that moment that it wouldn't matter. He would take her up because he wanted to, and look in the mirror the next morning with equanimity, knowing himself a good and law-abiding man. She was a villain, after all, scum from the Barrio. There had to be something she was guilty of.

Her feet were telling her to start running, but her accomplices were still out there, and if she just took off without them, they'd never catch up. Rationally, she suspected they were actually quite nasty and capable of looking after themselves, but that didn't stop her feeling protective.

Belly Keach was distracted, half lured off by the butter-salt aroma of a corn-seller doing business across Red-fountains. Lynx probably imagined he was watching her with the legendary acuity of his namesake, but he was so fond of picturing himself as the keen hunter that he tended to keep sentry with his mind's eye turned inwards on his lean calves and martial poise, rather than his real eyes on his quarry. And Lucas had just enough of the law to him to have to ease himself into taking her up, given she was just standing there, bandying words with him. When she ran, it'd be different, of course. Running was guilt, to the Broadcaps. Their few scruples got trampled underfoot mighty easily.

"Come on, Moppet," Lucas said. "Don't make this hard."

In the Siderea, the high town where the wealthy few lived, people went by their own names. The upper ranks of the merchantry and the magicians themselves, all the way up to Shorj Phenrir, who had been Archmagister of the Convocation for two human lifespans and still going strong. They had family names and personal names, dynasties and immutable identities. They got to be themselves. Everyone who belonged below the Siderea got a nickname, and that nickname came to define them and would go on their paupers' gravestones in good time. Still, Coppelia would dearly love to find out who had first coined *that* one for her and poke the worthy in the eye. Then she felt something run up her spine under her out-size shirt, enough to make her shiver. *One, and two.* Both her little friends repatriated with her, and a tiny hand knocked on her shoulder blade, also one and two. *Time to go.*

She gave Lucas Maulhands her sweetest smile and then bolted, just as he was waiting for her to do, the two puppets trailing by their strings after her, makeshift stage and empty hat abandoned. Behind her, Maulhands barked out a hard laugh, a man released from a residual ethical quandary, and she waited to see what devilish magics her accomplices had worked up to save her hide from the lash and her soul from the workhouse.

There was a colossal splash, unexpected enough that she skidded to an ill-advised halt and looked back. Lucas was in the fountain she'd been performing against. For a moment, she thought the carven marble nereid there was trying to drown him, which would have been the sort of working that the Convocation would hunt her for across a thousand years. Then she recast what she was seeing as something less undine and more mundane: they had laced his boots together.

Belly Keach was trying to haul the Catchpole out of

the water, and doing more harm than good, but Lynx locked eyes with her and broke into what he probably thought was a dynamic and predatory lope, but looked to Coppelia more like a tuppenny mummer impersonating an elderly cat. She took to her heels over the Lancemill Alley bridge that put her three streets from the Barrio and didn't stop running until she was in the shadow of the slum district's leaning walls and tattered awnings. And didn't stop her brisk walk thereafter until she was in the peeling upper room she called her studio, listening to the shouting of the family below and the bells of Beggar's Chapel from two streets away.

~

Too close. No bed, and only one stool, but she had paid too much for Szorca, the live-in landlord from the ground floor, to haul up a shabby mattress, and now she collapsed onto it. There was just enough movement in the straw to suggest a new deputation of fleas had come to make demands of her, which meant she'd have to douse the damn thing with Doctor Losef's Most Efficacious Paint Remover and leave it to stink out the street from the open window, or else spend the rest of the summer bitten by the little bastards. And Loretz fleas were a risky business. A flea that bit a magus might carry all sorts of maladies to its next repast. You heard stories, watered-down versions of the tales the doxies told, from when Convocation lords came slumming it to the fleshpots of the Barrio and left behind more than a handful of coins and a wet spot on the sheets.

"You might as well come out," Coppelia said. The meagre burden of her accomplices had vanished from her shoulders the moment she got in, and she knew they must be somewhere amongst the woodworking tools or the paints. They didn't fully trust her yet. She'd only been working with them a month, and their partnership was unorthodox, to say the least. Still, they'd trusted her with their existence and it had been safe so far, not another word breathed, not even to her fellow gutter scum.

There was a rattle from the workbench, one of her small wood files rolling towards the edge, and she lunged forwards to save it from the floor. They weren't good tools, not anything her parents would have been happy with, but in lieu of that lost set she remembered from her childhood, they'd have to do. They were charity from Auntie Countless, meaning a gift that Coppelia was still repaying day to day, given to her so she could do the work Auntie needed doing. Any breakages, she'd have to make good from her own pocket.

And, of course, that displaced file was no accident, and her grab for it put her on the right eye level for her little helpers as they stood on the bench top.

There were more than two of them, of course—she reckoned at least six lived up in the attic space above her studio, and probably more by now because, of all things, they were interested in recruiting. These two were the ones who'd approached her, though: Tef and Arc.

They were very beautiful, to her eyes. They were horrible, too, but only in a way that uncanny things often are, and in Loretz, the magicians' city, one got used to uncanny things.

Tef was the smaller, at a shade under Arc's full six inches tall. She had let Coppelia study her under the magnifying lens, her androgynous body miraculously worked in wood down to the smallest joint, every finger articulated in miniature. Having seen that, Coppelia had been terrified of going near her for fear of clumsily damaging some part of her, but Tef never seemed to own to the fragility of her existence. She had been running about the feet of the crowd at Redfountains, in and out of their bags and up and down their legs like a veritable flea herself.

Her face was the most remarkable, for it was not just a puppet's mask, caricaturing a stock character's expression. Every feature and part was separate: brows, lips, eyelids, cheekbones, jigsawing together in countless ways to give her as much expression as any flesh-and-blood woman. Coppelia could not do the faces: that was work left for Tef and her people, as were the hands. The rest was within her skill, though, and that formed the basis of her peculiar arrangement with their kind.

Arc was taller, broader and considerably heavier. She had a strap under her shirt for them to cling to, and she always knew which side he took because he dragged, and dug his pointy knees in painfully. He was made of steel, and not quite as intricately as Tef. His face was still cast in a dozen pieces, but his expressions were limited. He had a straight razor folded and slung over his shoulder, which she didn't remember him going out with. Arc was a warrior ready to take on the world. Why, once, he'd spent an hour duelling with the most monstrous rat she could imagine, so he'd told her at length, showing scratches on his metal torso as though they were battle scars.

"That was too close," she told them candidly. She took up her real puppets, the inert ones with strings. Simeon had survived miraculously untouched, but the other one, her all-purpose interlocutor, was hopelessly tangled, and she started the long work of separating all the threads. "At least tell me you have something to show for it."

The poise of the tiny creatures always amused her, though she'd never show it. Tef stood with her shoulders back, chest out, miniscule hands on her wooden hips. Arc tended to hunch forwards as though he was a big man in a small room, his gleaming hands bunched into fists like knuckly nail-heads. Taken without their surroundings, you'd think they were seven feet tall each and the greatest warrior-magi in the world.

Tef was hauling a sack up, meaning Coppelia's spare belt pouch. Upending it, she spilled a litter of junk over the bench-top: cheap-looking rings, a pendant, some coins, a quill pen, a carved wooden mouse clutching its tail in a frozen picture of rodent anxiety, a simple stuffed doll in a floral dress that was larger than Tef was. The jewellery would fence for a few coins, enough to make rent, but the rest looked like tat unless you had a touch of magery about you, like Coppelia and the homunculi both did. Enchanted stuff, nothing that would warrant a saga or a name, but worked with power nonetheless. Charms of protection, of luck, of sexual potency or relief from stomach cramps, all the little toys one could get in the middling markets of Loretz, that the city's merchant magi exported to the rest of the world at such prices.

"Let's dole them out, then," Coppelia said. She wanted to lavish praise on them as though they were pets, but that would be a mistake. Pets didn't carry a straight razor and secretly invade human cities. If anything, she suspected she was their pet more than they were hers.

But the haul was good. She'd have something to sell—maybe she could get some new paintbrushes this time—and they would have something with which to do ... what they did. And she'd better get on with her part of that, because that meant she could put off thinking about what might happen if she and they ever parted ways. What with her being the only human who knew about them.

Tef's jigsaw face was smiling, but Coppelia knew that didn't have to go any deeper than if she'd carved a happy face on one of her regular puppets. She'd have nightmares about that razor, that was for sure.

Later, when the pair of them had vanished off to the rest of their kin and Coppelia had settled down to assemble the pieces of a miniscule body made to Tef and Arc's own scale, some anonymous well-wisher pushed a note under her door. On it was a skilful sketch of a plump-looking woman along with a few spidery lines of description, telling over a life of wealth and privilege Coppelia could barely imagine. She left the little figure incomplete, because this was a paying commission from Auntie Countless, and Auntie was always in a hurry to get things done.

2.

ONCE UPON A TIME, there was a mannikin, a little figurine of a human being crafted by a great magician. What
this first homunculus was made from, nobody knew,
though Tef was personally certain it was wood, that perfect balance between durability and ease of working. And
the magician, by dint of his ingenuity, exposed this mannikin to a source of magic, perhaps in one great flash of
power, perhaps gradually over days or weeks or years.
And when it had been sufficiently empowered, it turned
its head, with eyes of paint or gems or buttons, and be-
held its creator, and found within itself a mind not unlike
his own.

Tef remembered coming to Loretz that first time. At
night—always at night, even though they could hide in
human boots and pockets. They came in on the backs of
ravens, birds from the Tower of their birth, grown tame
over long generations of husbandry. At first, Shallis had
wanted to guide them to where the magic was, that great
palace of domes and spires which dominated the Siderea
on the high ground away from the river. But night had

never come to that palace, a thousand magical lamps banishing the darkness so that the beautiful, elegant humans in their enchanted clothes never quite slept, either, but drank and sang and listened to unearthly music from instruments that played themselves. The homunculi circled high above that riot of life and excess and knew that, motherlode or not, they would never remain hidden where so many lanterns were kept burning. And so they sought out other places, darker places, where the humans crept like fugitives or slept uneasily behind thin walls. And there was magic even there, of course, because this was Loretz, where the magicians lived, and even the poor had some baubles of enchantment. But stealing from those who had next to nothing was both unrewarding and less likely to go unnoticed. So, the lines of their new colony were drawn: they would live *here* where the sharp senses of magicians might not sniff them out, but their hunting grounds would be *there,* on the other side of the river, where a magic mirror or an ever-sharp knife or a pair of shoes that danced for their wearer might go missing and rouse less of a hue and cry.

In one of the grand squares of Loretz was a statue of a man, a great magus, not quite the city's founder but from an early generation of alumni. He had been born there, been great, the sort of magician who, the stories said, destroyed armies, rode a brass-bodied dragon across the skies, raised the Convocation's palace from the dust in a single night; the usual. And then (though the regular story put a rather more heroic gloss upon it) he had got into some protracted disagreements with his peers about how the city should be divvied up, and in the end, he had taken his toys and gone away, never to be heard from again. There were even legends about him coming back to save the city if it was ever threatened, because the mage-lords of Loretz loved their myth-making, especially when such myths exalted their peers of ages past.

Tef had seen that statue and known it for a good likeness, for she had looked upon the original. Arcantel, his name had been, and he had obviously grown as sick of the company of his fellow human beings as of magi in particular, for he had gone far from the haunts of his kind, to raise a tower in a far and gloomy forest, where he had worked his magic for the amusement of nobody save himself.

And among the feats he had accomplished there, without distraction or rival, had been the creation of the first homunculus, Tef's earliest ancestor.

And then he had . . .

Well, there was a growing division of opinion there. Back in Orvenizzo, the human city Tef had visited before they followed the trail of magic here, the colony leader had been a staunch orthodoctrinist, clinging to the idea that Arcantel had so loved his creations that he had rooted himself in his ritual room in his tower's upper floor, making of himself a font of eternal power that his new children could use to infuse more of their own kind with magic, forever and forever, for that was certainly the fate of Arcantel. Barring disaster, he must stand there even now within his magic circle, staring at who knew what, hands out and fingers crooked in mid-wrestle with the powers of the universe.

That had been the orthodoxy for generations and generations of the made-folk. The Folded Ones who kept and taught the lore of magic, the great varnished lords of the Woodmen, the polished metal chiefs of the Sculls, the most embroidered Fabrickers, the Candle Kings, all the leaders of the different tribes of homunculi had told each other that the thriving and diverse civilization they had built within the walls of the Tower had been *meant*; their maker's plan.

But now they were out in the world, that unthinkably vast place where they were the least significant things imaginable, it was hard to believe in a universe solely aimed at bringing into being such minutiae as they. Tef didn't think it, and even Shallis, the Folded One who led the Loretz expedition, was half-hearted when she preached the creed. The world was too great, too complex, above all too *human* to sustain that belief in their privileged destiny. What Arcantel's motivation had been when he first imbued his little figurines with life, Tef could not say, but she believed he had not meant to end up a fixture in his ritual room to the end of time; he had not meant a thriving culture of made-people to grow up about his frozen ankles; he had not meant any of it, and whatever meaning they could lay claim to came from their actions and not their mythology.

Arc certainly thought so, but then, Arc had a lot of thoughts that were as far from orthodoxy as he could get.

Hauling her sack through the cluttered attic spaces they had made their own, Tef heard Arc ahead, already bragging to the others about what they'd accomplished. Not that he'd lend a metal hand in bringing up the loot, of course. She came into the Beetle Chamber to find him in mid-poise, steel arms flexing as he pantomimed drawing the razor from the pocket where he'd found it. To Tef's mind, Moppet's puppets had more artistic flair, but Arc was never one to be told anything. He exasperated Tef because he was a Scull, and everyone knew that Sculls were dour and brooding and usually violent, assured of being made of stronger stuff than just about anyone else, even if they would rust for a pastime if they didn't keep themselves oiled. Arc was not dour. Arc did not brood, although he was not entirely a stranger to violence. Arc considered himself an aesthete. On the other hand, Arc was stronger than she was, and willing to take more risks than the others, which meant that when it was time to go pilfer some trinkets, the job usually fell to the pair of them. They only had seven in their colony right now, after all. Nobody else amongst them had the temperament for larceny.

The colonies were new. Tef had been born to the Tower, though she had passed through five human cities before coming to this one. Each such city had a tiny clutch of homunculi living in its heart now. After centuries of isolation, the little made-people were spreading themselves through the world by stealth, establishing themselves wherever they might be able to scrape together enough magic to animate more bodies. It was a ruinous thing, in a way. They had hundreds of years of history and tradition that were teetering, a tower from which the bricks were constantly being robbed to build elsewhere. The vast majority of Tef's kind would rather none of it had ever happened. It was nobody's first choice.

But humans had come to the Tower, treasure hunters who had pried at the wards sealing Arcantel's ancient doors. At first, they had been taken for demigods, kin to the beloved maker. Only at the last moment had the homunculi realised that the humans had come only to rob the place of treasure and magic.

So opened this new chapter of their histories, because where one party of humans had come, so might others, in greater numbers and not so readily dealt with. And if the Tower fell, the entire long civilization of the homunculi would tumble with it, as though none of them had ever been. Faced with that, the magicians who guided them had decided they must go out into the world, spread their eggs from basket to basket so that if the worst happened, some might survive.

Of course, the greatest stricture in any of this had been that they must keep themselves utterly secret from the eyes of humans.

Arc's clowning died a death when Shallis came in, and his audience found other things to be getting on with. The Folded One glowered at the two of them out of her creased paper face, yellow-white and crossed with loops and spatters of Arcantel's own writing, a page from his long-neglected magical texts torn out and pleated into the shape of a stylised human.

"Let's see it, then." Shallis's voice sounded like she looked, the dry rustle of disintegrating things. Folded Ones lived a long time back at the Tower, where they did not need to expose themselves to the destructive forces of inclement weather. What had inspired Shallis to hasten her own demise by joining this venture, Tef couldn't guess. Her half-hearted lip service to the tales of Arcantel-the-Benign-Creator was probably at the heart of it. Hard to see such a stern, sour creature as a seeker of novelty and wonder, though.

Tef proffered the sack, and Shallis's origami hands spidered over the opening, hooking it wide so she could peer inside. She made a cracked sound, unimpressed. "And your human took the choice pieces, no doubt."

"An equitable division of spoils," declared Arc grandly, which at least meant Tef escaped the Folded One's baleful scowl. She could probably have let the Scull take all the disapproval, but that would just give Shallis more leverage to pry at their arrangement with the Moppet, which Tef was invested in. She sighed, just a little creaky noise in her throat, and waded into what was becoming a tiresomely familiar argument.

"We got more than we would have done, just the two of us skulking around," she told the folds of Shallis's back. "She makes a good distraction. And there's the making she's doing for us."

Shallis rounded on her with a hissing rattle that had Tef backstepping rapidly. For a moment, the sharp edges of the Folded One's frame were limned with cold magic.

"Well spoken, knothole," Arc murmured, in his hollow *sotto voce* that could be heard in the next room. This, of course, was the most unorthodox of unorthodoxies, and Shallis didn't like it.

Still, Tef planted her feet and held her ground, meeting the paper magician's glower head-on. They had talked over it, all seven of them, once they understood what they'd found in this Loretz place. They had weighed the crutch of tradition against the rope of opportunity, and though Shallis said they'd hang themselves with it, Tef had talked the others round.

Back in Orvenizzo, back in all the other towns and cities Tef had seen, each colony was built around a central hub. It might be a hollow in the earth beneath some floorboards, a wasps' nest abandoned and dusty in a neglected shed, a high shelf of a locked cupboard. In Orvenizzo, they had set up in the clapperless bell of a derelict church, building downwards in an intricate spiral of ramps and flooring. The hub was where they brought the magic, though: those trinkets they had found or stolen, sniffed out by their own diminutive magicians. Tef remembered how it had been, up in the bronze dome of that bell, the meagre heap of gewgaws and tat that still held some whiff of enchantment, and beside it, a single body, lovingly crafted from scrimshaw and rare woods, with brass mountings at the joints. Tef had never seen such a well-made body, and she could follow the magic seeping into it, using the sorcerer's skills the Folded Ones had taught her in the Tower. *Seep* was the word, though. Standing in the captive presence of Arcantel would bring a homunculus to life in a flash, so that access to him was carefully restricted and ritualised by long-standing tradition. That elegant shell in Orvenizzo would not stir for perhaps six months. Tef understood they'd had the new generation awake recently in Tello di'Bois, the little forest's-edge town that the homunculi had come to first after leaving the Tower. Slow, though, so very slow.

Here in Loretz they already had a hoard of magical bric-a-brac greater than all the other colonies put together, enough that word had spread and raven-back ambassadors were arriving with entreaties to share the wealth. Which would happen, obviously, but for now, the Loretzi colony needed to get on its feet and start birthing new colonists.

She hauled her hoard of ill-gotten gains from the Beetle Chamber (named after the menace they'd had to evict on arrival) and into the larger space beyond, the Blue Lantern Room. The lantern itself was one of their first magical appropriations, forever glowing with a dull azure radiance. Heaped around it was their hoard, and Tef turfed out her gleanings to add to the pile.

There was a body lying there, and soon to wake by her estimation. It was competently made, but its father, Lief, had been in a hurry. They'd brought no empty vessels here and assumed they'd have plenty of time for the work, not anticipating the bounty this city would provide. Loretz's first new colonist would live her life under the shadow of their decision, but it was that or waste their time when every new pair of hands was invaluable.

But the homunculi were small, and they made things slowly, taking pain over every joint and curve. They lacked the leverage and strength of a human, to master materials and swiftly bring out the latent limbs and features hiding within a block of wood or a mass of clay. Back in the Tower, a parent would craft a body over years, a labour of love to bring a child into a busy world. When the colony plan was decided, nobody had thought about the logistics of their miniature expansionism.

Faced with an embarrassment of magic in Loretz, they had endured seven days of paralysis as they tried to work out how to make best use of it, and then Tef, always the explorer, had discovered the shabby little workshop beneath their feet, and Coppelia, the Moppet.

3.

THE MAGIC WASN'T IN bringing the face out of the timber. Coppelia could do that at age six, even before her parents came to Loretz. She had the woodcarver's eye, to look at a featureless thumb of wood and see the shapes within it, what might be brought out, how the grain and contours of it might be tamed, a frontierswoman mastering an undiscovered country, until it would perform for her, taking on whatever shape her deft hands desired. Or perhaps there was a little magic in it: theirs was a talented family, in that way that made them unpopular elsewhere. The trades in most cities were governed by the guilds, after all, and the guildmasters were not magicians, and had no wish to give over their power and preeminence to those who could exceed their merely mundane capabilities. Which was probably fair, Coppelia considered, because they had children to provide for and needed to put food on the table. But at the same time, it was harsh, because those who turned up and showed any talent beyond the natural were kept from any decent commissions or just run out of town. And she had a sly suspicion that more than one guildmaster hid magical fingers within their expensive fur-lined gloves, their prejudices not truly against the arcane as much as against the outsider.

So, perhaps there was a little magic in the way she could whittle and shape the softwood to so resemble the sketch that Auntie had sent her, but the real magic came at the end, when she laid sculpt and sketch side by side and gave of herself to let the one infuse the other. Auntie employed an artist who was similarly a half-mage, who could look at a subject covertly and then make a likeness on paper that carried some of his model's essential nature. The sketch alone would not hold power long, though, or bear what Auntie would do to it, and so enter the Moppet, she of the abhorred nickname, to immortalise the work in wood and lend her power to it.

In truth, she'd rather be working on her other commission, the secret one for her upstairs neighbours, but Auntie paid. Moreover, Auntie was in good odour with the Barrioni, the criminal kings who parcelled out the Barrio between them. So long as Coppelia kept Auntie happy, Auntie was her shield against the knife-edged politics of the thief-lords.

As she was finishing up, fixing the carved head to the neck of one of her standard bodies (female, robust, suitable for comedy duchess or devoted nurse), a familiar presence impinged on her and she smiled. "Hello, Tef."

The little wooden figurine had been sitting with the half-made puppets and spare parts on the shelf above her workbench, as still as her unliving neighbours. Now she hopped down, feet landing with a precise *tok.*

"This isn't for you, sorry," Coppelia said, as the homunculus walked around her handiwork, head cocked on one side and her intricate face thoughtful. Unnerving, yes—all those pieces made it seem as if she was feigning the flayed, musculature exposed to view—but fascinating, too. Coppelia loved to watch the expressions chase each other across Tef's features, each one instantly recognisable despite its miniature canvas. "There are a couple almost done, though." With her elbow she indicated a pair of figures held in clamps, drying. One male, one female, not puppets but the articulated artist's mannikins that were always her first love, and the finest and most complex she'd ever built. Save that their wrists and necks ended abruptly, because the homunculi didn't trust her for that work.

Still . . . "I did a hand. Just to see. I used all my Craft." Meaning magic that let her go beyond the limits of pinvice and magnifying glass. Tef strolled over and looked at the result, spreading her delicate fingers to shadow it, finding Coppelia's handiwork close on twice the size. "Hmm." Like a branch creaking in the wind, so faint it was barely audible.

"I'll get better, if you give me the chance," Coppelia told her. "Or . . . I was thinking, could you be bigger? Because there's plenty of material. I could make bodies twice the size, or . . ."

Tef adopted a thoughtful pose, hand on hip, hand on chin. The body language of the homunculi always seemed slightly exaggerated, as though to make up for their size or the limits of their articulation.

"I think we do well, being small enough to hide within your hood or shelter behind your heel." Her voice was precise, not as high as one might imagine. She was almost shouting to make herself heard clearly. "Make us twelve inches from head to toe, we'd not stay secret long." She sat down, one hand waving away general exasperation. "Besides, that's an argument we don't need right now. Arc is already full of stupid ideas about what we should apply ourselves to. And Morpo wants us to try and animate a raven body, so we don't need to rely on living birds."

Morpo was made of wax, Coppelia recalled, a sagging figure who complained constantly about the summer heat, and would doubtless find the cold made him brittle. Coppelia was constantly amazed at the variety of the homunculi, even though Tef said this was but a mean sample of her home, wherever that was.

"I could do that," she mused. "I could make it from wax paper and balsa wood, lighter than the real thing."

"Don't start!" Tef called. "Don't encourage any of them! All very well for some Candling to say we should have a bird, but what about the newborn who wakes up to find out they *are* that bird, eh?" She threw up her hands theatrically. "Shallis says when will they be ready?" A thread-slender thumb jerked towards the drying mannikins. "Actually, Shallis says we shouldn't be doing this at all, but if we are, then when?"

Coppelia hadn't met Shallis yet, nor was she in a hurry to, given Tef's account of the presiding homunculus magician. "I can have one done for you when I get back from delivering this to Auntie. The other, I want to redo the knee joints. They're not as smooth as I meant."

"You've made them different shapes," Tef observed, on her feet again and inspecting.

Coppelia had to lean in to hear her. "Yes," keeping her own voice soft and low out of consideration. "One male, one female. Is that all right?"

Tef laughed. "No, but seriously." Then looked up at her, hands on tiny hips, body tilted back in surprise. "That's not how it works."

"I..." Coppelia didn't know what to say. She knew Tef was a *she* from Arc's referring to her as such, but all the homunculi seemed to be entirely androgynous to the eye. "I'm sorry, I just..." Tef's manner didn't suggest she'd breached some dreadful taboo, just that they were talking about very different things.

"I'm here!" Even as she thought through the implications, Arc bounded onto the workbench, striking a dramatic pose with his razor held high.

"Arc, what is that on you?" Tef demanded.

"What? I am magnificent, am I not? And the string-people she makes dance around all have clothes just like humans, and we are somewhat of a size." Arc modelled the gauzy white gown he had apparently abstracted from Coppelia's puppet sorceress. It should have looked absurd, but somehow it lent his self-important pomp a perilous grandeur. "We're going with you, also," he added, and the razor was abruptly an inch from her nose, his metal face like a tiny death mask.

"*I'm* going with you, to see this Auntie of yours. To learn more about how your city works," Tef said hastily.

"*We're*," Arc corrected. "And also, Shallis thinks you're going to sell us out."

There was an awkward silence in which Tef glowered at him and Coppelia ordered her thoughts. "I would never," she said at last, having methodically hunted down and extinguished all of the hurt his words had sparked in her. "But I understand. Please tell Shallis I do understand. Of course you can come. And if you have questions, just ask afterwards."

Arc nodded sagely. "Well, I trust you, even if the others don't." The razor was still extended, though, and he rediscovered it with an overstated double take before folding it and slinging it into a cloth scabbard he'd strapped to his back, over the gown.

Tef wasn't clowning, though, or even pretending to. "Why," she asked, "would you never?" She sounded as though it was a thought experiment or something similarly distant, not the future of her entire community.

"We help each other, don't we? I'm a good maker and puppeteer but only a passable thief. You're my light fingers." And Coppelia gave Tef a grin she didn't feel, because the truth would make her sound mad or false: that, as a marionette maker, the homunculi were the most perfect, beautiful things she had ever seen, even though they were frightening and unnatural. The child in her, and the artisan as well, had fallen instantly in love with their workmanship. She felt fiercely protective of them, savagely proud that they *had* trusted her enough to reveal themselves. But that, as Auntie would say, was the crazy talking. Speaking of which... Coppelia took a deep breath. "Well, I'm done here, and Auntie will be wondering where I've got to. If you're coming, let me get the strap and you may as well hop on." She went and wriggled into the leather harness that sat uncomfortably under her shirt. It was time to see Auntie Countless.

~

Her real name was Magda and, like well over half the Barrio's residents, she had come to Loretz from elsewhere because she was a half-mage and had thought this was a good place to get rich. Unlike many others, she had well and truly found her niche.

Auntie Countless was a collector, not of anything in particular but just of *stuff*. The homunculi were doubtless horrified by what they glimpsed of the woman's parlour. Coppelia understood that the basic ingredients of making were scarce, where they came from. They lived in a world on a very different scale, where even human poverty could represent an absurd largesse. Auntie lived surrounded by shelves and sideboards and occasional tables and none of them with an inch of space free from ornament. Auntie's tastes were catholic, not confined to the sort of conspicuous consumption that the mage-lords of the Convocation might indulge in. Everything was tat, much of it was twice broken and inexpertly glued back together: wooden fretwork, macramé, porcelain figurines, music boxes with dancers caught in half-leap, there were individual items that would have fetched a thousand ducatti from the right purse, and others that a scullery maid would be forgiven from throwing out the window in disgust. At the centre of it sat Auntie, doing her level best to look ancient and frail. And probably she was ancient, but Coppelia had seen her put a crab-apple fist into the throat of a bravo so hard, the man spoke hoarsely for a month.

Coppelia entered at her call, catching the old woman shaving, holding up a hand-mirror with an elaborately painted reverse as she moved the razor in deft strokes Arc could take lessons from. A pot of foam jostled the wooden pig family on the table beside her, the brush balanced precariously on its lip. Auntie could have kept servants, but she didn't trust anyone enough to share a roof with them.

Coppelia waited politely, the mannikin in her hands, aware of furtive shufflings beneath her shirt as the two homunculi crept to her collar and peered out. To her alarm, the cold metal presence of Arc began to spider his way down her sleeve, and probably he'd cut his way through the elbow if she didn't let him out. As nonchalantly as she could, she leant against a shelf crowded with plates, feeling him squeeze past her cuff with the barest rattle of crockery.

The sound flicked Auntie's eyes up from the mirror, and she gave Coppelia a broad smile. Her teeth were of black lacquered wood and Coppelia could smell the enchantment off them from across the room. "Dear heart, always such pleasure," she got out, her voice husky and low. "Come, sit, take tea with this old woman."

There was always tea, when Coppelia came, as though the nonexistent servants had just departed. It was a bitter brew nobody else in the city drank. She wove through the clutter and displaced a wonkily taxidermied fox to sit, then carefully poured out the steaming green liquid into a pair of mismatched beakers. Niceties done, she set the mannikin and her instructions down for Auntie's inspection.

Auntie Countless's talents did not lend themselves to crafting things, or even to infusing them with magic. Whatever traditions held sway in her far-off home were a vein of magery untapped by the Convocation. In Loretz, they had made her a blackmailer *par excellence*. As hers was a trade that leached only off the wealthy, was of sporadic use in the schemes of others and would allow potentially spectacular revenge if anyone crossed her, she commanded some respect in this parish of the Barrio. If she'd wanted, she could have been a thief-lord herself, Coppelia suspected. Auntie never seemed to want anything more than comfort and more stuff, though.

The sketch and description from Auntie's artist would be of some middling-wealthy woman, one of the merchant magnates who made a comfortable living hanging about the waist of the city: above the scum, below the true mages. Coppelia's work had built a link between the figurine and its living exemplar, but that was as far as her own skills went. Auntie's sorcery would let her exploit that link, influencing the woman's actions in countless little ways, discovering secrets or, if the woman turned out to be improbably blameless, prodding her into doing regrettable things she might wish to pay money to prevent being discovered. All of which was surely very wicked, but Coppelia found that, in Loretz, sympathy was like water: you couldn't push it uphill very easily.

Auntie looked the work over. She tended to drop the just-a-dotty-old-woman act when she was exercising her magic, and her gaze was steely-keen. Coppelia was horribly aware that right now, Arc was somewhere at large in the room up to who knew what mischief, but so far, the metal homunculus hadn't kicked a porcelain kitten off a sideboard or done anything else to draw attention to himself.

"This is fine work," Auntie Countless declared with another black-lacquer grin. "You improve, dear heart. You've a knack for it." She looked past Coppelia's poker face and her expression creased. "I know it's not what you wanted as a trade, accessory to this old woman's nasty habits, but follow your gifts. Momma Nasty puts food on the table still, since Poppa Nice cleaned out the cashbox and went to live with his mistress." And she fixed Coppelia with a stare that dared her to flinch or look hurt. Auntie had been one of the first to find her on the streets after her flight from the orphanage. The old woman had seemed a cruel taskmaster at the start, for years even, but every day, she had been working to toughen Coppelia up. She'd made the girl her long-term project, armouring her fit for life in the Barrio. Now she nodded grimly. "Good for you, dear heart. And this is master-level for a little Barrionette like you." *Barrioi* was the formal term, for a denizen of the Barrio, but Auntie liked her jokes. "I have some rich friends I can introduce you to, who will value your talents almost as much as I do. Once we can agree on commission, of course."

Then a heavy fist was pounding on the door. Coppelia jumped but Auntie just froze, one hand abruptly out of sight down the side of her chair, where some weapon must be concealed.

"Why, I'm just painting my face, dear heart!" she called. "Whoever's come calling?"

"Paint it any colour you like, won't help worth a damn!" a man's voice barked. "Message from the Iron End."

"Arses and tits," Auntie swore tiredly, rolling her eyes. "Come in, sweetling. Come tell this old woman what's so important." She still had her hand hidden, and the other clutched at her chair's arm so that the blue veins stood out.

A man stooped in, tall and rangy, wearing a leather jerkin with a lining sewn with metal plates. Coppelia knew his long, lean face: a crooked nose and ginger stubble and eyes that bulged enough to make him seem permanently furious, when in fact he was famously calm about his trade. He was Kernel, called Jointmaker, not for any work with lathe and plane but because he tended to leave his victims with more than the usual complement in any given limb. He was also chief bully-boy for Gaston Ferrulio, the gangmaster who lorded it over this parish of the Barrio. It was a testament to Ferrulio's power and respect that he had gone through eleven years of calling himself the Iron End and nobody had ever found it funny to his face.

Kernel eyeballed her, and Coppelia shrank back from the obvious recognition on his face. You didn't want Jointmaker to know who you were, because he probably didn't have many casual acquaintances, only targets.

"Convenient," he grunted. "Auntie, Himself wants to see you. And you can take your hand off that pig-sticker or whatever you've got down there. Something's come up in your line of work." He squinted at Coppelia again. "This your puppet-maker, this is Moppet, no?"

Auntie lifted her chin, facing the man down with dignity. "Whatever this is, it's no business of hers, sweetling."

"Oh, it is. You think the Iron End doesn't know just

who owes him? Time for her to pay rent on the air she breathes around here."

Coppelia was frozen, because what could Ferrulio possibly want with her? She'd have bet the gang-lord didn't even know she existed, but probably her work for Auntie had slowly percolated up through the ranks. She was a criminal, after all, even if a petty one. A criminal living within the domain of a greater criminal. Probably this day had always been coming.

"When, and what for?" Auntie asked, all the "sweetlings" gone from her.

"Tomorrow. Noon. Bring an empty stomach. Himself's partial to dining with his honoured guests." Kernel made it sound as though they were being cordially invited to their own executions. "What for? His business. Not mine to tell." But then he cocked a sneer at Coppelia and added, "He's got a puppet problem, you think?"

"Do I . . . need to bring anything? Samples, prentice pieces . . ." Coppelia couldn't force her voice above a whisper. *A puppet problem.* And did that mean her secret—the homunculi's secret—had got out?

"Prentice . . . ?" Jointmaker's protuberant eyes goggled at her. "Just bring your hands, girl, and hope you still have the same number of fingers when you leave." He laughed unpleasantly—but then, he did everything unpleasantly—and slouched out of the house.

"Arses and tits," Auntie Countless said again. "Dear heart, it's either go to dinner with the wolf or move out of the woods, and I am too old to pack a bag." Her gaze took in the teetering memorabilia on all sides. "You, on the other hand . . ."

I have nowhere to go. And the homunculi . . . Again that surge of affection for them, such tiny motes of animation in a world ready to crush them at every step. "Noon tomorrow."

4.

"WHAT DID YOU TAKE?" Coppelia had felt Arc slip from beneath her shirt the moment she got up the stairs to the studio, but he wasn't quick enough to get into the attic before she turned around. She caught him frozen in furtive flight, halfway up the shelves he and Tef used as a ladder. Under his arm was . . .

For a moment, she thought it was actually another homunculus, but then her mind performed a brief inventory of Auntie's cluttered parlour and she recast it as a figurine from a musical box, gold or gilded and about Arc's own height. Tef had extricated herself by then and was shaking her head. If Coppelia had a magnifying glass to hand, then doubtless she'd see the wooden homunculus's eyes rolling.

Arc straightened his shoulders and placed the figure down on its feet, still rough where he'd pried it from its mounting. It was a dancer, the limbs elegantly articulated, the face one piece and locked into a cold smile. Looking at the workmanship, Coppelia had a sinking feeling that Arc had made off with the most valuable thing Auntie actually owned, because she reckoned it was gold, and the glitter in the thing's sculpted hair and the lines of its meagre costume was crushed diamond, if she knew anything about it. There was a lingering enchantment about the figure, sharp in her nostrils, that suggested it had danced with more grace than mere mechanisms could have given life to, but right now, parted from its box, it was nothing but a diminutive trophy.

"She's beautiful, isn't she?" Arc put an arm about the figure companionably. "Eh? Why not, then? We need the bodies, don't we?"

"*He,*" Coppelia corrected absently. "And—"

"*She.* If I finish her and give her life, then *she,*" Arc pointed out, as though she were stupid. The dancer was definitely crafted as a very well-endowed man, but that obviously wasn't the point.

"Look at its face," Tef pointed out.

"Well, we'll need to give her a new face, obviously." Arc waved away the difficulty, smiling fondly at the dancer's fixed expression.

"There are rods and gears in it."

"We'll open her up and take them out."

"Shallis won't go for it. Arc, we're both pushing her patience as it is. This isn't how things are done." Tef was practically begging. *Don't embarrass us.*

Arc scowled, the expression played for comedy on his simple features, but Coppelia suspected the sentiment was real enough. "I couldn't ever make a daughter this fine," he muttered. "And Moppet does wood. We don't have some tame human goldsmith or steelworker. And I want a child." And Coppelia had to turn the situation on its head again because she'd been thinking of a man wanting a mate, but of course why should that even be a consideration for the made-people?

Auntie will notice he's gone, she thought. *She. It. Notice that it's gone.* But even so, she said, "I'll find somewhere to hide . . . her. While you work things out with Shallis."

Arc beamed. "Thank you kindly, Moppet."

"Don't—" she started, and Tef said at the same time: "She doesn't like that." The wooden homunculus cocked her head. "What now, then? We're all thinking the same thing about this Iron End creature?"

"He wants to mess with us, I'll give him *my* iron end," Arc decided, the razor out for more brandishing.

"Ferrulio is powerful. He runs all the streets around here. Nobody makes a brass tornese in this parish without his nod."

"Maybe we can work with him," Arc suggested. "Maybe he wants an introduction."

"He doesn't know about us," Tef insisted. "He can't."

"Maybe we're not as clever as we think we are." His

weapon stowed, Arc folded his arms. "What's your design, M— 'Pelia?"

Run? But she had a living here, pieced together under the noses of the Convocation, built from nothing and held up by a scaffolding of contacts like Auntie. She made money, she had debts she could call in, and she had access to magic as she would in no city else. And this was the city that had taken her parents from her, which meant it was also her last link to them, terrible though that was.

And maybe Ferrulio knew nothing, and she could brazen with the best of them, a face fit to win card games.

"Could you just leave, if you needed to?" she asked them.

"We could." Tef shrugged. "We'd lose all we've built. And if the word really is out, we'd have to abandon this city. And maybe word would spread. Better to be under a thief-lord's thumb in secret for a while than have all your kind spreading stories of the little people living amongst them." Coppelia could fill in the blanks. Access to Loretz's magic was more important for them than for her.

"We can't make the decision alone. We need Shallis and the others to speak their piece. But if you go, I think we'll ride with you, to listen to what this Iron End has to say," Tef guessed. "And if the worse comes to the worst, we've killed humans before." It was something Coppelia would expect from Arc, who'd make it all bluster and bombast. From calm, mannered Tef, the words were chilling.

~

The Barrioni gang-lords fancied themselves sophisticates. Was this not Loretz, after all, where learning was king and the greatest magicians of the age ruled the sunward side of the city? Should their opposites and equals be any less urbane and elegant? That *equal* was entirely within the minds of the Barrioni: they shared out the city's meanest district for their stamping grounds and constantly tested the boundaries set by the Convocation without ever quite breaching them. But within the Barrio, their authority was life or death, and they feuded constantly to see who could be king of the most nothing.

Gaston Ferrulio, who exalted in the nickname of the Iron End, was one of the youngest and simultaneously one of the strongest: ambitious, pushy, heedless of traditions that let his seniors sink into decadent complacency. At thirty years, he cut a trim figure, thin face barbered to a point and wearing a robe of green slit down the middle to show well-turned legs. He was known as a duelist in his own right, lucky in games of chance, farsighted in games of strategy and absolutely the worst man in the Barrio to make an enemy of. Standing in his presence,

Coppelia could barely look at him for all the magic he was festooned with: rings, pendants, brooches, belt buckle, ear stud, even the bone beads in his long hair were enchanted. This was what it meant to be rich in Loretz, even rich on the wrong side of the law. No doubt he had protections against every poison, against blade and bow and all manner of assassin's tricks. If it were easy to kill a Barrion, then Ferrulio would be dead a hundred times over.

He held court about a great gilt-topped table that itself was a repository of magic, probably scrying by Coppelia's guess. His underlings had at least put in the effort to look like courtiers rather than thugs, but few of them had any success approaching that of their master. Kernel Jointmaker, when he took his place at Ferrulio's right hand, looked like an ungainly peasant. But then, he wasn't exactly retained for his social graces.

There were precisely two seats free at the table, both all the way down from the Barrion himself for which Coppelia was profoundly grateful. It wasn't that the Iron End was a ruthless gangster; it was that he was suave and handsome and drew the eye just like a polished knife does. She preferred her monsters to look monstrous.

In anticipation of the Barrion's magical accoutrements, she had already dispensed some stern words to Arc about the foolishness of making off with *anything*, no matter how much it might suit the homunculi's cause or his personal taste.

Auntie Countless was not a stranger to Ferrulio's presence, though Coppelia could tell the old woman was on edge. Still, she bowed and then curtseyed, one companionable hand on the puppet-maker's shoulder, and they sat when the Barrion waved a languid finger towards the vacant chairs. Coppelia hunched her shoulders in. There was a broad, pig-like man on her left who was surely a child-murderer, and on Auntie's far side was something not remotely human, a bloodless-looking man-shape with huge owl eyes, a slit of a mouth and no nose at all, dressed in brocade and velvet like a merchant on feast-day. The crouching presence of Tef and Arc beneath her shirt only made things worse, because surely some mage or half-mage would wonder what kind of enchantments an orphan could have acquired and want to take them off her. Except everyone there had a few magical trinkets on them and nobody spared her a second glance, barely even a first one.

Coppelia wanted out as soon as possible, because she felt the axe hanging over her, waiting to see if Ferrulio would suddenly start talking about little mannikin people stealing on his turf. Apparently, business amongst the Barrioni wasn't done like that, though. There was food first: fish with lemon and cloves and thyme, little pastries full of chillies, tiny minced-fruit tarts that reeked of rum. She had never tasted anything like it before, just as she had never worn fabrics like Ferrulio's fine robe, or had the use of a room as grand as his dining chamber.

The Barrion himself ate sparingly, picking at each dish, exchanging bons mots with the woman on his left, and sometimes telling jokes that were obviously at Jointmaker's expense and which made the enforcer glower down at his plate. And then, even as most of his guests were still mauling their dinner, he clapped his hands together, and apparently, that meant business.

"Let's talk about puppets," he declared, and for a horrible moment, Coppelia thought she was intended to put on a show for this audience of killers and thieves, and of course the only mannikins she'd brought had minds of their own. But Ferrulio kicked back in his chair, slinging his pointy-shoed feet up onto the tabletop, and gestured. "You're known for a certain way with the little wooden mummers, Auntie, and we hear some promising things about your Moppet there." It was the first time Coppelia had been glad of the name, because it meant Ferrulio wouldn't be speaking her real one. "You'd call yourselves experts, then? Willing to look into a piece of business for me?"

Coppelia found herself gripping the table edge and made herself stop. *"Business" meaning little people getting where they're not supposed to?* She tried to smile, feeling the expression stretch and deform on her face. Auntie was sweating a little, even without a burden of guilt to dampen her, but she bared her black teeth and said, "Barrion Ferrulio, my sweet, this old woman has forgotten most of what she ever knew, but between us, we can put on a creditable show."

Ferrulio grinned, and when he turned the expression on Coppelia, there was a moment when she liked him, when it was just he and she, and he was laughing at the fakery he had to put on for the others. Then it was gone, leaving her chilled by how suddenly she'd been won over. "Why, then, Auntie, I have a puzzle box for you to open, because one of mine has come across something quite intriguing while going about her business."

Here it comes. Coppelia could feel her heart hammering, out of her control. Then Tef's tiny wooden hand stroked down her shoulder blade: the lightest of matchwood touches, but it meant solidarity of a sort. It calmed her, just a little.

"Shabby, if you'd regale us," Ferrulio said to the woman on his left, who stood with liquid grace. Shabby Lilith Yarney had either cleaned up well since acquiring the name, or else it was like calling a big man *Tiny*. She was a pale woman with raven-dark hair in spiralling plaits, wearing a white neckerchief and black boots and her fine clothes every shade of grey in between. Coppelia knew her by name as a burglar of the first water who plied her trade well beyond the safe borders of the poor districts.

Her voice was pure Barrio, cheerful and coarse enough to set Ferrulio wincing. "We had an in-'n'-out job up top on the Siderea, certain mage-merchant's townhouse where the cellar got dug too close to the old Semper Chapel grounds, what used to be up there. Crypts're still down below, though, aren't they. Only a bit of chisel work to be in amongst the good stuff." She grinned, three silver teeth throwing back the light. "'Cept we got lost as buggery down there and, next blush, we was out in some other place none of us knew, all buried down there, tunnels for miles. Well, Rosso wanted to bail, but I——"

"Perhaps on to what you actually discovered," prompted the Iron End.

"Right, chief. Only, we worked out we was under the palace, right enough. And we found some decent swag, just lying about all covered in dust but magic as you like. And we found a workshop."

Coppelia's ears pricked up, because this was definitely moving away from homunculus territory and into guilt-free areas of interest. By her side, Auntie was very still, meaning very thoughtful.

"All kinds of tools and benches and stuff, for wood and metal, mostly fine pieces. I reckoned it was jewellers, maybe some smiths the nobs had nabbed to make their fine tiaras," Shabby went on. "Only, there was a hand there, like a metal hand, all the fingers and bits, big as mine. And there was a frame, like you'd stick armour on, if you was a nob and wanted to show off. And Rosso came back sharpish then, and spooked to arse and back. There'd been a man, he said. A man of metal, jointed like a big old puppet, just standing there. And we were both freaked by then and we legged it with what we'd grabbed."

"A fascinating tale," Ferrulio drawled, obviously wishing it had been told with a little more showmanship. "It would appear one of our betters in the high city had a little side project, now or in times past. Certainly not one nosed about in public, which, given how servants overhear and how they talk, means either long forgotten or very secret indeed." He seemed very sure that, in the normal run of things, he'd know what was going on. "And what about that for a thought? A mannikin the size of a man, not just some puppet or music-box toy. What do you think?"

Coppelia stole a guilty look at Auntie, but the woman was intent on the topic at hand.

"I think nobody has even tried to animate a true golem since Arcantel," Auntie declared. "And even he achieved only doubtful success, if you read the true histories. I think many have tried. Archmagister Phenrir himself was about it, decades ago, so this old woman hears, and maybe this is his failure, or maybe it is some competitor's success. I think that such a thing, if it could even twitch, would command a king's worth should some enterprising young blade get it out of the city to sell. Or some other Convocation magus would swap half his trove of trinkets for the chance to learn the secrets of its manufacture." She sucked at her lacquered teeth noisily. "I think you thought the same the moment you heard this nice young lady's story, but I think you reckoned, not so easy to get out of the mage-lords' cellars with a life-sized statue. And then you started thinking about how a golem is just a big puppet, in a way, and of certain of your subjects who have talents in that direction and might be able to get it to stir its stumps. Has this old woman torn out the guts of it for you, your honour?"

Ferrulio, his thunder if not stolen then at least reduced to a few closing rumbles, nodded grudgingly. "Auntie Countless, your perspicacity has always been your most noted commodity, and here you have an apprentice with a young pair of legs to carry a cupful of your wisdom when Shabby here goes back with a proper crew to get the job done. What do you say?"

Coppelia was gripping the table again, because the whole conversation had just dropped into free fall as far as she was concerned. *I am not a thief.* Although she was, of course, just not in the same league as Shabby Lilith Yarney. She couldn't just . . .

"It's good of your honour to worry about my infirmities, but for this, I would crawl on my knees if I had to. The girl can help me and be my hands, but these old eyes aren't so tired they don't want to look on a real golem. If that's what there is, and not just some mage-lord's self-praising statue." She cocked a look at Shabby and the thief shrugged.

"Rosso said it had joints and all. Didn't see it myself."

"Do I take it you'd be willing to assist in a little venture, Auntie?" Ferrulio said. What struck Coppelia was that he did actually ask, and with every indication of respect, even though the old woman was just a moderately successful grifter and he was lord of all the shadows he surveyed. And if he hadn't needed Auntie, then doubtless he wouldn't have pissed on her if she was on fire. *And* he wasn't asking Coppelia herself, doubtless written off as just some tributary creature of Auntie's. But the courtesy was still there, however shallow. She was horrified to find herself actually warming to Gaston Ferrulio, and that was a very unwise thing indeed.

"Let's talk terms, your honour," Auntie said, her black grin widening.

5.

"**THIS IS HUMAN BUSINESS**," Shallis told them both. "You risked enough going before the thief-lord. If he hadn't been blinded by his own finery, he'd have found us."

They'd all gathered there in the Beetle Chamber. Its floor was a pan, its ceiling poked with holes to let in the moonlight. Effl the scrimshander had caught some fireflies, in that way she had to sneak up on living things effortlessly. Now the tethered insects battered and buzzed about the upper reaches of the room like a maddened candelabra. All very well, but someone would have to clean away the worn-out husks come morning.

"And what then? We'd just be taken for toys of the Moppet," Arc pointed out. "They have so much here. Why would they care that she has some magic dolls? Eh, Tef?"

The wooden homunculus shook her head slowly. "It's not like that. You'd think it would be, but it's not. Because they have plenty, do they share it around?" Tef went on. "This city is ruled by magicians who hoard their magic.

The poor are ruled by thieves who hoard gold and what magic they can get. Anything the human girl has can be taken from her."

Shallis coughed, a dry, rustling sound, quiet and yet enough to demand silence. "And yet you trust this child, even though she's human."

Tef rolled the joints of her shoulders. "I do. You've seen the bodies she made. They're good work."

The Folded One's expression creased inwards. "When there are more of us, we won't need to rely on this . . . hired help."

"When that day comes, perhaps we'll have a deal in place with the humans anyway," Tef countered. "I'm not saying they're all our enemies. Probably most of them we could get along with, even. But the ones who control things, they're bad news." Her features clicked into a bitter expression. "No different to how it was in the Tower. My father's mother was all splits and splinters by the time I took life, while the Varnished Lords live on in perfection because they kept all the riches for themselves." She glowered about, ready for dissent, but then none of them was a thing of gilt or gold thread. The rich lineages had stayed where their power was, in the Tower. The colonies were for the adventurous poor with nothing to lose.

The whole colony had come to hear her and Arc's recounting. Lief had his knees drawn up to his wooden chin, hands still working on a piece of hardwood, carving the segments of a thumb almost absently as he listened. Morpo slouched against the wall, relishing the night's cool, the firefly light gleaming greenish from his wax body. Beside him, coiled in a heap, was Kyne the Fabricker, resting her elbows on the serpentine coils of her stuffed body. Across from the pair of them, with a definite space around her, was Effl Ratkiller, a creature of intricately scrimshawed animal bones, spidery and delicate, polishing the fish-hook end of her polearm. Finally, there was Lori, sitting silent beside Lief and trying to copy his pose. She had been alive for precisely half a day, and Lief was working hard to teach her everything she would need to know. She had no words yet, and every movement was as though yanked by a palsied puppeteer. She was the first Loretz native among them, though; the first of many, they all hoped.

"The workshop of the Maker!" Arc declared, arms spread wide. "We know this is where he came from, before he built the Tower. We've seen the statue, or some of us have. Arcantel, they call him. Centuries later and they still remember how mighty he was. And now some gutter thief has found his workshop, surely! What might we learn from it, even if this golem is just fancy and shadows?"

"Enough!" Shallis hissed, waving crinkled paper hands.

"Enough from you, empty-headed Scull! Tef, you agree, then, that we should let this business alone for humans to meddle." She was their magician-leader, their font of wisdom, but there was a scratchy note of whining in her voice. Too many changes, too many deviations from tradition. Shallis's page had been torn from a magical book, but without the strong spine to support all this pressure.

And Tef felt sorry for her, and wanted to reassure her, but there were other considerations.... "I will go," she declared. "Whether this is what they say it is, I will go. And like Arc says, maybe this will be a whole new lease on life for all of us, for all our kind." She didn't believe it. Something rang wrong about the entire business.

"This is because of your human, the puppet-maker," Shallis accused bitterly. "You would betray our presence here for the sake of your pet."

Tef thought about outright denial, but unlike Arc, she was ill-suited to the theatrical gesture. "There are ten thousand humans in this city, hundreds of thousands in the land beyond. Millions, maybe, in lands past our ken. And each one could crush any one of us without even noticing. Each one lives surrounded by material goods beyond our comprehension and thinks themselves very poor. And here we have one, just one, who has kept faith with us, these months, and worked for us, and not sold us to the thieves or the mage-lords."

"Whose domain she is about to venture into," came Shallis's hollow, fearful voice. "And of all the humans, if *they* should learn of us . . ."

"All the more reason we go along to keep her safe."

The prospect of Tef and Arc being able to keep a human safe from other humans was too much for Shallis to countenance and she just rattled her edges against each other, throwing up her hands in disgust before stalking from the chamber.

"That's settled, then," said Arc brightly, straightening the gown he'd taken from Coppelia's marionette and adjusting the hang of his razor. "The workshop of the Maker it is. Secrets!" he added, hands out to frame the idea as though it were a portrait. "Wonders!"

Effl cackled shrilly, mouse-skull head turned to goggle at him. "I heard your words of what the humans said. Rust-head, knot-hole, what fools you are! No word of dust to a human's knee, no word of cobwebs like thick curtains? The Maker left here hundreds of years ago, and you think this place is *his*?" She stalked up and jabbed Arc in the chest with her spear, tearing the gown and leaving a bright scar. "Some other mage is making puppets, fools. And think what a gift you'd make for him!"

~

Auntie sipped her tea, gazing thoughtfully at Coppelia, come to call on the old woman after sleeping on the Iron End's request, which was to say *demand,* and half-expecting to find her packing her most precious of trinkets to run away. Instead, the old woman was ensconced in her armchair again, in a pensive mood.

"The mage-lords," Auntie said softly. "You know, some people think they're not human—not now or not ever? That they live, breathe and shit magic; that if they wear a shirt, that shirt is big magic by the time they hand it off to the laundress?"

Coppelia nodded.

"You believe that, dear heart?"

"I believe they must be great magi. But that's a long way short of gods."

Auntie cackled and slurped her tea. "Back home, we had a game: how long we could keep a spy in this city." Coppelia's eyes widened, because this was opening doors on the old woman's life that had been shut before now. "A city run by magicians! What's not to keep an eye on? Until we worked out the game, and then we lost interest. Still, a good way to prepare a retirement for when the home guard changes and you need to beat feet out of town." She gave Coppelia a sly look. "You want this old woman to tell you the secret? You're probably as much a magician as half the Convocation. *I* most certainly am.

Oh, there are a few who are exceptional, the old ones who've burrowed into that palace like grubs. Our puppeteer is like that, I'd wager. They say Phenrir really is a bigshot magus, and he keeps his fancy chair by exploding anyone who tries to take its soft cushions. Two centuries on this Earth, dear heart. You'd think he must have learned something in all that time."

Coppelia nodded. She could not imagine the reclusive Archmagister Phenrir as anything other than an abstract concept, any more than she could stare into the heart of the sun. He had not left the palace in a lifetime, nor even his chambers, they said, ruling all Loretz from their shadows.

"So, maybe he's half the mage they say he is," Auntie allowed graciously. "But the rest . . . not talent, not personal power, but they have the *stuff,* dear heart. Staves, crowns and gems, enchanted spoons and querns that turn corn into bees and all that other nonsense. The good stuff, that we never see, not even Gaston Ferrulio. It's not skill that makes them mage-lords. It's a fat inheritance, is all. So: no different to any other city, save the nature of where the power comes from. And now some gutter-runner of our parish has gone and found a crack in the wall where the rats can get in." She drained her cup with relish. "And this old woman's not so infirm she can't be a rat one more time. How about you?"

Coppelia, who had been hanging her nose over her own cup without much enthusiasm, started at the question. "Me?"

"You want to fall sick, rush to the bedside of your ailing grandmother, some other excuse, I'll make it wash with the Iron End. You don't have to go."

Coppelia stared at her. "What?"

Auntie's expression was sombre, as old as the rest of her face for once. "You're a gifted one, dear heart, and too sweet-natured by half for the Barrio, and yet you made something of yourself that isn't a victim. So, this old woman cares a little for you. Not a lot, but then, I don't have so much care in me as I used to."

"I'm going with you," Coppelia said, more to stop the confession than anything. Auntie was wizened and sharp as a crab apple, and that made her the person Coppelia liked to visit. Genuine aunt-like sentiment felt oddly threatening, ties that bound her. Besides, whatever this caper meant to Auntie or Shabby or the Iron End, to the Moppet it meant something important to her diminutive house guests. Hearing the thief tell over what they had found and seen, she'd felt Tef and Arc tense as they clung to the strap. Whatever the mage-lords had been attempting in that workshop, it had been akin to the tiny rituals the homunculi were about in the attic, infusing life into the inanimate.

"I thought you might be," Auntie said. "It's your parents, of course."

Coppelia choked on the tea and spent a good minute hacking it out of her lungs. When she could stare at the woman with watering eyes, Auntie Countless was nodding sagely.

"Taken from the workhouse, you said. Because they stole or failed to meet quota or got into fights, or because no other reason than they were taken, because who questions the Convocation? And some say they die, who get taken. Some say their magic gets drunk up by the magi, to make up for their own inadequacies. But they're artisans, in the workhouse. They have skills the mage-lords don't. So, maybe they get taken for other reasons."

"You think they're ... still there?" Coppelia could hardly breathe. She hadn't thought of any of this. The idea had never occurred to her.

Auntie shrugged and poured herself more tea from a pot that never seemed to run out. "Dear heart, this a city of magic, haven't you heard? Anything's possible."

6.

THEY ASSEMBLED BEFORE DAWN outside the Bag of
Teeth, a tavern as unsavoury as it sounded and a place
that Coppelia would normally never approach of her
own volition. For Ferrulio's people, though, it was the
landmark of choice that everyone knew when it came to
getting the crew together for a heist.

She had thought the Iron End himself would be there,
for some reason, seeing off his valiant underlings with a
gracious wave. Except staying abed until dawn had broken was probably a privilege of rank, and most likely he
didn't want to see any of them until the business was
done.

There were six of them: a large crew for a heist, even
if two were only along as special puppetry advisors. Coppelia discovered that, at least as of the dinner and war
council with Ferrulio, she knew all of them by sight. The
thought made her obscurely proud. If she was a thief, as
she most certainly was, then this was her world. It did
her good to embrace it by learning the nicknames of its
luminaries.

Shabby Lilith Yarney was most definitely in charge. She wore the same monochrome palette as she had at Ferrulio's elbow, but the cloth was all hard-wearing canvas and calfskin and serpent-belly scale, and her white neckerchief was now a scarf she could pull up to hide half her face, enchanted to keep out evil odours and poison gas. She was loose-limbed and at ease, standing there in the gathering grey and counting them off, exchanging a few grinning words with her old cronies as they pitched up, nodding with respect to Auntie, cocking an eyebrow at Coppelia.

The girl tried to meet her gaze, but couldn't quite. Shabby was elegant and beautiful and confident, a legend within the parish. Coppelia, *Moppet,* was just a kid who made dolls.

Shabby's confederate from her previous errand, Hamfingers Rosso, was tearing into a fresh-baked loaf for makeshift breakfast. He was a balding, broad man whom Coppelia had seen about the parish, drinking and brawling and arguing, chaos at his heels wherever he went. Here, he was very still, nodding warily to Auntie. A cudgel lodged in the belt that strained against his broad belly. His shirt was open halfway to his navel, a window onto a gnarl of greying chest hair. Incredibly, Hamfingers was the name he'd been born with, and he'd earned "Rosso" from the rosy broken veins of his drunkard's nose. Now he inclined his head to the next comer. This was the creature that had been Coppelia's neighbour at dinner, and she shuddered still at the sight: lipless mouth, huge circle eyes.

"Doublet, my man," Rosso greeted him, and the thing clasped his wrist with pallid, nailless fingers.

"Rosso, been too long." Doublet's voice was a whisper. "Mik bottled it, then?"

"Came down with a case of being stabbed on the swanny." And that was all the requiem Rosso had for Mik, whoever he had been.

"There's a lot of it about," Doublet confirmed sepulchrally. He was dressed in dark red slashed velvet, a beret balanced rakishly on his hairless head. There seemed to be nothing of magic about the creature, and Coppelia had no idea what his purpose amongst them was.

Last to arrive was a more familiar face. Doctor Losef was a well-known name across half a dozen parishes, invoked whenever fever, constipation or impotence reared (or failed to rear) their heads. He was also purveyor of the paint remover that Coppelia had found to be so effective in keeping off fleas, and was a source of various other forms of alchemical comfort. She hadn't known he moonlit as a thief's assistant, but apparently, he had many strings to his greasy bow. Sweaty Losef, as the street named him, had more than a touch of the batrachian about him: a broad-mouthed, smooth-skinned man with bulging eyes and a slight rainbow sheen to him, his collar and cuffs always sopping and stained. She was used to him in an apron or apothecary's robe, but here he was dressed in shadow-shades like any second-storey man, brown stockings showing the spindly shape of his legs and a bandolier of pewter flasks across his chest.

"Not keeping you waiting, was I, lords and ladies?" Losef's voice was professionally unctuous. "All accounted, are we?" He took Shabby's hand and moved it to within an inch of his rubbery lips but didn't touch. His own hands were hidden in stained leather gauntlets, because Sweaty Losef was his own alchemical laboratory in times of need, and as such he avoided contact with human skin unless he meant to send a powerful message.

Rosso had a stack of smocks, the dung-brown hue given to the menials who swept Loretz's streets and mended gates in those parts of the city containing people rich enough to matter. Not the Barrio, therefore, but the mercantile districts this side of the palace wall saw their attentions from time to time, and most of them came from the workhouses, drawn from the host of immigrants come to find a better life in the city of the magi. These were the meanest of the workhouse crews, though, those without the skills to craft or enchant. It meant they lived in poverty, looked down on by everyone, but they probably weren't vanished away without explanation much, either.

Coppelia thought about that as she struggled into the ill-fitting, stained garment. The official story was that those in the workhouses should be very grateful for the chance to work with minimal pay for the city's overlords, and that one day they would become citizens or even magi if they proved themselves. And everyone knew someone who knew someone who was a big wheel now having come from the workhouses, though nobody seemed to know that second someone directly. The story that got told round and round was how much of a privilege it was to get a workhouse place, and how it was perfectly just that those who abused the generosity of the Convocation should get taken away for ... various fates. Exile sometimes, execution, imprisonment. Fates that meant nobody heard from those people again, and the rest of the city closed ranks to say that they had deserved it. Until the people who got vanished were your own parents and you suddenly realised that your place in the orphanage was now doubly earned because you were genuinely an orphan.

And once her eyes were opened she worked out that the bulk of those who got vanished were promising artisans or half-mages or both. Thugs and petty larcenists of lower status might get pilloried or whipped by the Broadcaps, but they didn't just go missing overnight, never to be met with again. And yet, no matter how obvious the conclusions seemed to Coppelia, the bulk of the city blithely went on telling the same old stories of justice and just dessert, because to do otherwise might be uncomfortable. That was another reason she'd taken to Barrio life so well: people there were less interested in propping up the Convocation with every word they parroted.

The dung-browners certainly got to cross the palace wall to go "up top" into the Siderea, because some tasks were too menial for anyone to invest the magic to sort out, and even magicians needed to use the crapper. Everyone knew that the gates were always watched and the crew chiefs' faces were known to the Broadcaps and marked with magic. It was no shortcut for any thief wanting access to the riches of the palace district. Probably, Shabby and Rosso had scaled the wall or some similar piece of midnight daring, but Auntie Countless was certainly not going to be hoisting up her skirts and climbing a rope anytime soon. Nobody on the crew seemed concerned, though, and Coppelia just pattered along behind Auntie, hoping that somebody had thought things through. On their way out of the Barrio, the conversation was mostly about division of spoils based on some system whereby Ferrulio would get certain choice pieces, after which everything would get broken into shares according to arcane rules of seniority and specialism. Coppelia, as puppet-inspector's apprentice, got a half-share and didn't feel bold enough to argue.

Then the houses around them were of better repair, the early-morning travellers of a less-villainous and -hungover caste, and they were leaving the Barrio behind them and moving into Fountains Parish. Shabby halted them then, one thin finger raised for attention. "No more cant," she said flatly, all business now. "We're dung-browners on our way to muck out some mage-lord's dunny. Look miserable, look humble. And Doublet's our crew chief."

The owl-eyed creature gave a small bow. Coppelia goggled at him, because surely the Broadcaps on the gate were going to realise that this prodigy wasn't one of their regulars. Nobody else so much as raised an eyebrow, and so she held her peace and trusted to their experience.

Auntie must have marked her expression, though, because she cracked a black-toothed grin and said, "You watch and learn, dear heart."

They processed through the city, from the meanest districts to the prosperous parishes up against the Siderean wall, which would normally constitute the high-water mark of any prudent thief's attentions. Coppelia, who had plenty of experience in slinking about beyond the Barrio's edges and not being seen, was astounded at how unremarked they all were. Everybody knew the dung-browners. They went everywhere and they did the crap jobs, and the richer you were, the more beneath your notice they became. It was as though they were just another exercise of the Convocation's magic, that unblocked drains and replaced paving slabs by sheer invisible sleight of hand.

And then they were at the gate, with the Broadcaps, and that invisibility could surely not survive the glower of the Convocation's half-mage lawmen. Their Blue House stood just on the gate's far side, and Coppelia waited for Lucas Maulhands or one of the other regulars to stroll out and recognise her.

Doublet waved cheerily and strolled up to the Broadcaps on duty, his chain of followers shuffling at his heels. Coppelia was tense as a drawn wire, ready for this madness to fall over so she could run all the way back to familiar streets. The Broadcaps just exchanged a few words with Doublet, though, and one even peered into his face. Then the gates opened just wide enough to admit them single file, and they were filing right on through.

Doublet glanced back, just as Coppelia slipped in and the gates closed themselves quick enough to nip the hem of her smock. The inhuman face was gone, replaced by flat, comfortable-looking middle-aged features, complete with bushy sideburns and a prominent mole. That face met her gaze and Doublet winked one of its eyes deliberately, and still she had not a sniff of magic from him. Seeing her regard, simultaneously horrified and fascinated, he put a finger to his cheek and tugged down on it to expose his eyeball and the inside of his lower lid, a child's gesture of defiance from the orphanage yard. Except he kept pulling as though his flesh were just clay, opening a hideous trench down from his eye, the organ itself rolling in raw red flesh. Coppelia squeaked, and then Shabby cuffed Doublet across the shoulder.

"Stop messing," she told him, and he let his malleable features snap back, which was even worse.

Coppelia wasn't sure if there were any chapels still standing within the Siderea; it was rare for the magician-lords of Loretz to pay even lip service to gods. They encouraged it in their people, while ensuring that the primates of the various sects were well-enough looked after to preach the right sort of things about knowing one's place and accepting the proper order of things. Most of the city chapels had catacombs or tombs or just capacious wine cellars, though, and the demolished Semper Chapel had been no exception. A townhouse stood there now, property of some upwardly mobile merchant at last propelled over the palace wall by the momentum of three generations of double-dealing. The sight of brown smocks and the avuncular visage of Doublet convinced the haughty-looking majordomo that they should all be instantly admitted into the cellars, where the dung-brown smocks were doffed and stowed for easier access to tools of the trade.

"Doublet, good work, man," Shabby told him. "Coming, staying or going?"

"Wouldn't miss it for the world." The creature's huge-eyed visage was back, thin mouth twitching in nothing much like a smile.

Shabby and Rosso conferred briefly, and then they were opening up an already-damaged section of wall that the majordomo had probably thought them there to repair. Doctor Losef had some little clay contrivances like salt shakers, giving each a brisk flourish so that a dull red radiance guttered from their pores.

"Patented nightlights for everyone. Good for detail, doesn't carry. If consumed, see a doctor immediately." He gave a liquid chuckle and shared them out. Coppelia was aware of a distinct craning movement from the two little burdens on her harness. The homunculi didn't like fires, so perhaps Arc and Tef were intrigued at this new possibility for illumination. She managed to hook her little pot onto her collar so they could take a look at it if they wanted.

Shabby and Rosso led the way down, from cellars to the chapel crypts, from those, past broken walls, dry sewers and one leap over a crack in the earth that seemed to go down forever, into vaulted halls that must be the palace's own subterranean maze. Shabby was setting a brisk pace over ground already familiar to her, and soon Auntie was leaning, on her cane and on Coppelia in equal measures, to keep up.

There were a few close calls along the way. At one point, a half-collapsed ceiling meant they were passing beneath the feet and noses of a trio of Broadcaps, off duty and gambling in some neglected storeroom. Their rowdy cursing and banter rang every which way, coming back in mocking echoes as though there were enemies on every side. Auntie rose to the occasion that time, twisting a ring on her finger to conjure a haze in the air that would hide their movements from the distracted men above.

Another time, they dropped down into what must have been natural caverns, twisting hither and thither where the water had run in bygone days. Then it was the turn of Doctor Losef again, spattering their path with an acrid-smelling liquid, pitch black in the red light.

"Mewclaws," Shabby explained briefly.

Rosso chuckled at Coppelia's blank look. "You're thinking something like a lizard-cat-thing, right?"

She nodded cautiously.

"Well, that much is true."

Doublet tittered, a spine-chilling sound. "You're thinking they are adorable, girl-child? That much is not. Be glad the doctor's ichor smells worse to them than it does to us."

At the end of that, when they had hauled themselves up into the elegantly buttressed halls again, she pointed out that they'd not seen hide nor hair of anything like their Mewclaws, to which Losef replied that it only showed how good his repellent was, and she couldn't tell if he was making fun of her or not.

And then they were in a tunnel scented distantly of paint-stripper, or so Coppelia's nose could best characterise it, and Rosso was reaching up to a metal grate above, painstakingly unscrewing it from its stone mounting. Up there was only more darkness, but by some unspoken signal, everyone else seemed to know that they had arrived at the fabled golem workshop. Coppelia felt Tef and Arc crowding her collar for a look, cold metal brushing her left ear, the grain of Tef's head against her right.

Rosso slid the grate painstakingly aside and then Shabby boosted him up: he was a broad man but he wriggled effortlessly through, a professional about a job that only taxed him slightly. Then he was reaching down and hoisting his partner, and each one of them after that, with special care and consideration for Auntie. Last as always, Coppelia half-expected to end up left down there, one more joke on the newcomer, but they were all quiet and serious business right then. Rosso hauled her up one-armed and set her on her feet in a chamber large enough that Losef's red lamps did not reach the walls.

What they did illumine was a workbench that Coppelia was beside and goggling over without feeling she'd crossed any intervening space. Her own workbench in the Barrio was the result of years of scrimping, saving, handcrafting and outright theft, and she had thought herself quite the well-equipped artisan for her own small trade. Now she felt such a deep, deep jealousy, an envy of the soul like acid in her, because if she had owned something like *this*, then what might she not have accomplished?

Tef was right up alongside her neck now, hidden in her unruly hair, and no doubt the little homunculus was thinking just the same.

"Puppets, right?" Shabby said, and Coppelia started guiltily, but of course the thief meant the tools and not her diminutive passengers.

"Or something like it," she agreed, hearing her own voice shake. She saw vices, files for wood, for metal, for bone. She saw saws and pins and little heaters to keep the paint and the glue liquid while they were being used. And that thought led to . . . "But it's old. Not old like the walls of this place, but nobody's used this stuff within a month at least." Her own workspace smelled of that hot glue, the burnt odour of sawdust and sanding, the hundred little tells of an artisan at work.

Shabby shrugged, but to Coppelia it spoke volumes. Someone had invested a colossal amount in this place, all those bespoke tools and pieces, and then let it lie fallow. They had made their golem, perhaps, and then given up on the work, the consummate amateur with no need to pay rent or buy bread with the proceeds of their craft. On the heels of her envy came a fierce, unexpected hatred for whoever was behind all of this.

"No dust," Doublet remarked.

"Charms for that," Rosso and Auntie replied, almost in unison, and of course whatever dilettante crafter had set up shop there would never do something so menial as *sweep up* after themselves.

"Moppet, dear child, over here," Auntie Countless called, and Coppelia dragged herself reluctantly from the wonderful bench to view something even more remarkable. Here was another table, set with clamps and indentations, along with lathe, drill and bandsaw that all fairly radiated magic—no ungainly crank or foot-pedal here beneath the palace.

"Larger pieces," she identified, looking at the new toolset. Certainly larger than she'd have any use for, but if someone did want to craft a full-sized frame in exquisite detail, they'd need to work at all scales, from the minuscule to the human.

Rosso and Doublet had satchels out and were swiping anything that looked valuable—and there were wells of gold shavings there, pots of hydrargyrum, glass bottles of precious tints and colours, each one of them a year's earnings for any artisan that might want to acquire them. Doctor Losef was prowling about the edges of the room, a red lamp held high in each hand as he hunted for where Rosso had seen the golem.

"Moppet, Auntie, get the best glimmer you can of this place, what they did here, all that," Shabby instructed.

"They weren't making an army, or even a load of servants," Coppelia said quietly. Auntie watched her silently, but she sensed the old woman was of the same mind.

"What, then?" Shabby asked.

"Just one," Coppelia told her. "Look at all these precious metals"—now vanishing into Rosso's pack, but the point was there. "And nobody's making any more of them, not now they're done. Maybe they're just doing repairs to something they made a while ago, or something they found an age ago. No team of artisans churning out magic metal people. Someone came here and made something precious. And then they lost interest." But even as she said it, she felt it wasn't quite right, a pat explanation to salve the professional ire she felt, but the picture of the idle one-time amateur didn't quite sit right. The place wasn't as abandoned as all *that*. The left-over scents in the air suggested a little tinkering in living memory.

"But it was in this room, Rosso saw it," Shabby said, though there was doubt in her voice. "And I don't see it now." Even as she frowned, Sweaty Losef was hissing for them. He'd found a door, solid and bound with what might be polished brass or might be gold. There was a lock, but locks were Rosso's speciality and he had it sprung in a minute of picking and thirty seconds of half-magery.

Coppelia was expecting a storeroom, a broom cupboard of enchanted brooms, something mundane to the rich yet of vast value to gutter-level thieves. What they got instead was a bedchamber.

It was immaculate, that was her first impression. She saw desk and chair, writing paper and ink laid out; there were great velvet drapes shrouding what surely couldn't have been a natural window this far down but might have been a magic mirror or some simulacrum of a view. There were pictures on the walls, portraits of severe men painted to make them look powerful, of elegant women painted to make them look ethereal. There was a scene of a castle on a moor somewhere, stark against the flames of a volcanic sunset that shed its own burning red light across the room. On a side table, the orbs of an orrery danced without visible support.

She had eyes for none of it, not after she saw what lay on the bed. And it was a fine bed, too—a night's sleep on it would be worth more than every material possession she had ever owned: four-posted, with drapes tied back, the bedclothes heavy and worked with gold and mercurial thread. And lying in it, arms demurely crossed over its chest, was the golem.

Silver and gold, it was, and precious metals. Its face made Arc's steel visage look plain as the back of a spoon, so fine was the work. Its hair was a riot of moulded golden curls. Its body was perfectly in proportion, crafted not as a naked marionette but clad in coat, breeches and stockings, enamelled in red and black and imperious purple. Coppellia marvelled at the joints of its hands as they lay on its breast. *I am learning my craft just by seeing this.* The two homunculi were both at her ears, peering through her hair at this prodigy, and she was terrified the other thieves would spot them.

"See the power in him," came Tef's tiny creak of a voice. "Our work is done here already."

"What?" Coppelia asked. She had been lost in the wonder of the golem's construction. She hadn't been looking at the *magic* in it.

Then Rosso shoved past her, staring down at all that incalculable craftsmanship with the air of a professional with a practical problem.

"How much does it weigh, you reckon?"

Of course they were there to steal it; they were thieves. Still, a life-sized man of metal would be a challenge to abstract from the bounds of the palace wall, and every dent or scratch would rob them of more money than any of them had ever held at one time.

"Wait," she said. Only Auntie glanced her way.

"Stretcher, bandages," Doublet opined, rubbing at his face, which moved queasily under his fingers. "Say it got burned. Dung-browners have accidents all the time."

"No, wait," Coppelia said, more forcefully, because she knew the pattern there, the way the currents of power coiled and knotted within the metal frame. She knew it from the homunculi, though it was writ on such a larger scale.

"If a stretcher'll hold it . . ." And Rosso hauled down the bed curtains and all the pillows and covers that the golem wasn't actually weighing down, piling them on the floor.

"Rosso, no!" Coppelia got out, shaking off her paralysis to grab at his elbow. He shook her off irritably. Shabby and Doublet paid her more heed, but before either could intervene, Rosso laid hands on the thing to roll it off the bed.

It took his wrist. Rosso cursed, more startled than anything else, yanking away. And screaming then; screaming and on his knees because the golem had pinched with thumb and forefinger and separated the bones of his hand from one another, discharging magic flaring from the joints of its fingers. Above his agonised keening Coppelia heard a musical metal voice, dreadfully clear, crying out, "You dare?"

Auntie tried to stop her seeing what came next, or just tried to get her back through the door, which amounted to the same. Her eyes were fixed on the golem, though, as it swung its legs off the bed. It still had Rosso's mauled stump in one hand, and the other was thrust at the next nearest thief, Doublet. The malleable creature was tripping backwards, stumbling over Rosso's extended foot, and a moment later there was a flash of . . . not lightning, not fire, just magic, a raw discharge of the colossal power that made the golem go. Doublet made no sound as the top of him was just ablated away, a sharp line from waist to armpit the new boundary of that part of him which remained, the rest gone to dust and empty air.

Doctor Losef was already trusting to his heels across the workshop, having not gotten past the threshold of the door he had discovered. To Coppelia's surprise, he paused at the grate, a thief's residual loyalty remaining in him, for all he was a pharmacist and only an honorary villain. Shabby was right after him, sliding the last few feet and vanishing down into the space below. Rosso had been her partner for years, but she recognised a lost cause like any gutter-born urchin. Next came Auntie, trying to bundle Coppelia before her, and after her—

Coppelia saw it in Losef's froglike face: that the feet that came after hers were metal, not flesh. His nerve failed him then, for which she blamed him not at all, and he was down the hatch and after Shabby without another glance.

A gleaming hand fumbled for her, plucking at her sleeve, and she and Auntie spilled over onto the floor of the workshop in their haste to escape its reach. In two long strides, it was between them and the hatch, kicking the grate across the workshop floor. Despite herself, despite Rosso and Doublet, Coppelia winced at the bright scar left in the onyx enamelling of its boot.

"You dare?" it said again. "You dare creep into my personal chambers, you rats?" And its golden eyes rolled wildly so that she braced for the murderous rage a human would surely fall into.

She kicked back, retreating across the floor on her backside and heels until her spine rammed up against one of the workbenches. Auntie crouched before her, hands up, *surrender, let's be reasonable, please.* And the golem cocked its head in just such a way that Coppelia shivered, because the thing had been so painstakingly fabricated to resemble a man.

"Your honour," Auntie croaked, and then there was the sound of many feet, of shouting. Broadcaps came spilling over through the bedroom and into the workshop, a dozen of them at least, and behind them men and women, richly clad, who must be magi of the Convocation or their hangers-on. Coppelia recognised their looks from the orphanage and the streets: a veneer of concern over a greed for someone else's misfortune.

"Your honour!" Auntie shouted, hands reaching out to petition, and one of the Broadcaps just stepped past the golem and struck her in the head with his cudgel, a single, brutal motion that sent the old woman to the floor, her head haloed in blood the moment it touched the stone. Coppelia screamed, scrabbling away until a hand on her ankle yanked her back.

She'd thought the impassive regard of the golem was the worst, but then she met the Broadcap's eyes, finding an expression of such utter disgust, as though she was vermin, no more than a human rat crept in from the sewers; human loathing won out as worse than mechanical disinterest. She tried to kick him in the face, any victory no matter how small, but he got an elbow in the way and then rammed it down on her ankle.

There was a little flourish of steel about Coppelia's knees and then a lash of blood whipped across her cheek.

For a moment, she thought it was her own, but then she saw that Arc was standing on her legs, his razor extended in a fencer's lunge, and the weight of the Broadcap was gone from her, the man rearing back and staring at his neatly slit wrist.

She heard Arc's tinny little challenge, a tiny steel man trying to take on the world, but there was no future in that. She couldn't save herself, but she wouldn't let her downfall be theirs.

She flexed her knee hard, sending him cartwheeling off her towards the still-open hatch, skidding between the golem's very feet until he almost tilted in and fell. He was getting to his feet, though, razor still very much in his grasp. A single boot-stomp from any of the Broadcaps there would have turned him into nothing but broken parts.

"I'm sorry." And Tef was gone from Coppelia's other shoulder, bolting between the feet of the oblivious humans. The wooden homunculus grabbed Arc by the waist and just leapt, carrying the pair of them down into the dark.

Which left only Coppelia, the Moppet, but she felt as though she'd won something, despite it all. She'd stolen a treasure from these monstrous people who'd taken her parents and killed Auntie, and who owned all the magic in the world.

Two Broadcaps were moving on her, cautious because of the blade they thought she had. One had a cudgel, the other a proper sword; neither looked in the mood to take prisoners. Coppelia fixed the swordsman in the eye and bunched herself to spring at him, reckoning she could at least get her nails into his face before he could finish her off.

And then, "Hold," came the cold, clear voice of the golem.

7.

"**THEY SAW YOU.**" Shallis's dry, crisp voice out of Shallis's dry, crisp mouth.

"The humans?" Tef glanced at Arc, hoping that he would let her lead the narrative. "I don't think so, not really. We were quick, and they weren't expecting anything like us."

Shallis rustled, a living document impatient with circumlocution. "The construct."

Another glance at Arc, who was sitting on the edge of the pan that was their meeting-chamber floor, cleaning his razor and sulking. No help there. "Yes."

"That is also one of their magicians."

"Well, it could throw power around, if that makes it—"

The Folded One rattled her page-edges together, cutting off Tef's words. Around them, the rest of the colony leant in, unusually silent. Tef tried to gauge their mood, but just because her own face was wood didn't mean she could read meaning into the features of the others. Morpo's sagging wax, Kyne's button eyes, they were all simply watchful right now, still as only the unliving can be. If they'd had breath, they would be holding it.

"This is . . . problematic," Shallis stated at last.

"It was going to happen anyway," Tef decided. "This is a city of magicians. Even the street-sweepers know a few charms. We are creatures of magic, given life by it. Sooner or later—"

"Later, it was to be hoped," the Folded One told her. "When there were more of us. When we could maintain more than one hideout. When there were enough of us to threaten them, if it came to war."

"War with the humans? Are you mad?"

"If they set to eradicating us, the only way we could get them to halt would be if we had *teeth*. Half a dozen sad puppets in an attic? The work of a moment to destroy. A hundred of us, two hundred? When we could have a razor's blade at any nursery window, a pipette of hemlock in any cup? *Then* they would have to come to terms with us."

The silence that followed this proclamation was of a profoundly different nature. Tef glanced around and reckoned she could read them now, as shaken by Shallis's words as she was. "Is *that* where your mind's taken you? Poisoning and murder?"

"I . . . think about these things," Shallis whispered. She made an abortive gesture towards their own newborn,

Lori. "You think *they* would hesitate?"

"I think they would go a lot further to wipe us out once we started killing their young," Tef said. "Shallis—" She was expecting a sharp put-down, but instead, the Folded One just folded, collapsing until she was sitting, all angular misery and jutting corners.

"We are so few," she said. "When we left the Tower, how could we know how big the world was? How everything in it could destroy us, fire and rain and humans, humans, humans. And now they know about us, and this city does nothing but consume, devour all that is precious or magical to feed those who rule here."

Tef frowned, feeling her eyebrow and forehead pieces slide over each other. There was a thought there, if she could only grasp it. Thankfully, Arc chose that moment to come out of his funk and rejoin the discussion.

"You're all missing the point," he declared, flicking the razor closed and stowing it. "Both points, actually."

"And what would you say is the point, exactly?" Shallis demanded.

"The golem," Arc said, "was fucking brilliant."

The adjective was not native to the Tower, but he had been around a lot of humans. Tef had thought he'd been sulking, but apparently, something else had been going on in that metal skull.

"You didn't see," he pointed out to them. "You complain about Moppet making bodies for us, but these humans can *build*. This was a whole full-sized body made like us, out of the finest materials imaginable. Back in the Tower, we've been paring away our resources like that cheese Moppet has, making do with as little as possible 'cos there are so many of us. But here there's plenty, and we can be more. We can be big, or we can be fine, or we can be anything we want. You want to go make a deal with the humans? Make a human-sized one of us and get the magic to wake it. Make a thing like this golem."

"Are you *insane*?" Shallis demanded.

"Beats planning to kill them, and it's me with the razor telling you that," Arc pointed out jovially enough. "Look, this golem thing—"

"Won't be like us. Will be dangerous," Effl the Scrimshander said. "Will be just a toy to the magi, a real puppet. Like they'd make of us, maybe."

Another silence, and this one profoundly uncomfortable.

"What's your other point?" Lief, the other wooden homunculus, broke the silence. "You had two."

Arc waved in thanks, acknowledging the reminder. "Oh, right," he said. "We have to go rescue Moppet."

"*What?*" Shallis demanded, and Tef was thrown by this as well because Arc had kept his own counsel from start to finish.

The Scull wasn't remotely put off by the general in-credulity. "They took her. They didn't kill her like the oth-ers," he declared. "We heard. The *golem* stopped them. And she's our friend. She's one of us."

"No, you see, she isn't—" Shallis started, but Arc just bowled on.

"She made us bodies. She helped us get magic to power them. And she took us with her to that place be-cause we wanted to go. And she got me out of there when I was about to go sever some hamstrings. Well, she and Tef did. So, I'm going back there to get her out."

"Well, good luck with that," Shallis said disgustedly. "As they already know about us, I suppose when they catch you like a mouse, it won't damage the rest of us more than has already happened."

"Not on my own," Arc said. "Tef's coming, too. Aren't you."

Tef looked from him to the rest. *Am I?* And didn't she feel a bond to the Moppet, after all? Save that her thoughts were more on the golem itself, the implications of its existence. *Is it like us? Was it made by the same ma-gus?*

Even as she formed the thought, a hand seized their meeting room—no, the whole building—and gave it an angry shake, a dog with a rat for just one moment. Dust exploded from every seam, and the pan floor slipped from its mountings and ended up at a slant.

They poured out, half-expecting to find an angry mob of humans tearing the house down. There were humans coming out onto the street, certainly, but they were all exclaiming to one another, as baffled and frightened as the homunculi.

Out across the Barrio, streets away, a great plume of smoke was gouting skywards. Without a word, Kyne was slithering his stuffed-cloth body for where their ravens sheltered, off for urgent reconnaissance.

~

"This puts things in perspective, in a way," Lief said, after Kyne had brought the news back. At everyone's blank looks, he shuffled uncomfortably and explained, "It doesn't matter if you're human-big or like us. If they want to stamp on you, they will."

The gang-lord Gaston Ferrulio, who had exalted in the title the Iron End, was gone, as was the entire building he had taken as his headquarters, as were all his minions, petitioners, servants and casual visitors who had been unlucky enough to be present. A bolt of concentrated magic had launched into the skies from the Siderea and descended upon him with pinpoint accuracy, and now instead of a block of three-storey buildings, there was a hole that had burned the earth past the foundations, melting the ground itself into a shiny marbled patina.

We were right there, not so long ago, Tef thought numbly. The other homunculi were huddled in on themselves, gathered almost shoulder to shoulder, trying to draw reassurance from an empty well. Shallis stood apart, their leader, their own magician-lord, a scrap of paper against the storm.

"We need to get out of this city," Morpo said, his voice shuddering. "We leave. We find somewhere else. Another town, the barrow of some king buried with his magic sword, another tower, maybe. Yes, better somewhere without humans."

"This is where the magic goes." Tef hadn't expected Shallis to speak out against the idea. The Folded One was shaking softly, trembling like autumn leaves in the fall. "You saw the other colonies. They're all asking us to send them magic, even the meanest of half-mage nonsense, because this is where it all comes to. These magelords, they clutch it all to them, the material that could give birth to a whole race of our kind. We will never be many enough, spread enough, unless we can dig in here."

"Yes," Tef agreed. "And for that, we need the humans. As allies."

"We need Moppet back—" Arc started, but Tef waved him to silence.

"Humans? You've just *seen* what humans do when they're angry!" Shallis hissed.

"Yes, and they do it to each other. These people here, in this Barrio place, they are poor, and they take what they need from those who hoard it. That's what *we* do. We have more in common with them than they do with their leaders. And Arc and I have shown we can work with them, help each other. Profit."

"Just what are you proposing?" Shallis demanded, although there was a giving weakness in her voice, already acknowledging that she had lost control, perhaps that she no longer wanted it.

"We know some of them now," Tef pointed out. "And they just had their leader killed and their friends. We can go speak with them, reveal ourselves. Tell them that Moppet made us, maybe. And we can ask them for help, to save Moppet, and we can help them get revenge."

"You're choosing sides already." Shallis said disgustedly.

"You've seen the sides," Tef pointed out, to Arc's enthusiastic nodding. "Was there ever any doubt which of them we'd be on?"

8.

THEY HADN'T KILLED HER. She wasn't sure why; everything just threw up questions like a dog kicking up dust.

They hadn't killed her, because the *golem* had ordered them to stay their hands. The Broadcaps had blades and bludgeons out, and she was, what, not even a real thief worthy of their time, just a child too old for the shield of the orphanage to stand between her and life. And caught there, with the robbers in the mage-lords' sanctum. Of course they'd kill her, or at least beat her a bit before they hauled her off to stretch her neck as a warning to miscreant youth.

But the golem said stop, and they had stopped, not just the Broadcaps but the magi as well, those tall, elegant men and women with their enchanted clothes and jewellery and cosmetics. They had come to see a diversion, she thought, perhaps some misfortune visited delightfully upon a peer. They could have spent their magic and turned her to dust with the twist of a ring or the exhaustion of a bracelet. More economically, they could have had their servants club her to death or cut off her ears or any number of similar fates, an exercise of power that only increased its fountainhead rather than expending it. And yet the golem had spoken and they had listened: not creators to an object or masters to a slave. Not even equals, but inferiors. Not one of them had wanted to meet its burning golden eyes.

And from there it had been a short trip to this cell. It was one of some two dozen where a high-ceilinged subterranean arcade had been subdivided over and over into little plots barely a yard and a half to a side, but high enough that a slender man ten feet tall could have stood upright with ease. The floor was hard stone with a dusting of decaying straw. There were rats, or at least a rat had chosen her cell as its final resting place, and probably others would come to pay their respects in due course. There were fleas, perhaps also in mourning for the same late rat. There was no window or skylight, not there nor in any of the cells. However, some improvisational prison architect had chanced upon a dweomered statue, so she guessed. The whim of its enchanter had it glowing a cold green-white, and the architect had broken it into chunks and set one into each little square of ceiling. Coppelia's, by poor chance, had the face and one reaching hand up there amongst grime-obscured tiles of mosaic. She wanted to see the grotesque display as a fellow prisoner of the cell, but the unknown workman had placed the pieces to give the impression of encroaching motion, and she knew that, if she was able to sleep, she'd have nightmares and then wake to see it and have them all over again.

She found the most congenial corner of her small domain and sat there, head down, arms about her knees, and waited for the worst, knowing only that the world was not done with her yet. Perhaps her parents had done the same, in these same cells, years before.

What came next probably wasn't the worst, although it didn't make her day any better. The hatch in the cell door shunted open and someone rattled a cudgel in the slot to get her attention. Looking out in the statue-light, she met the eyes of Lucas Maulhands, Catchpole of Fountains Parish. Below those eyes and his sharp nose stretched a cat-cream grin that went all the way to his ears.

"Well, lookee," he drawled. "We caught a Moppet."

A burble of laughter from out of sight suggested he had an audience of at least one of his underlings. He fit his face into the square of the hatch as close as possible, the wooden frame denting his chin and brow, drawing as much sustenance as he could from the sight.

"Now, this is what comes of playing dress-up in adults' shoes, doll-girl," he lectured her. "You hadn't run, back when I had you, you'd have some stripes on your back'd remind you what your place is, and then you'd not have come to such an end. Now . . . a waste, Moppet. You took your little nugget of talent and tossed it in the river, didn't you."

Coppelia felt a desperate need to have some sharp comeback, to say Maulhands was a man who'd know about little nuggets, to taunt him that, even if she was caught, he'd had no part in it, to make suggestions about the size and activity of his familial tackle, even. Except the words froze in her mouth and she choked them back down, because she was there now. If Maulhands wanted to put the boot in, then the key to her door was just down the hall. He could take his belt to her, his fists or his club, and nobody would cry out, and she couldn't run anymore. Rosso and Doublet and Auntie were dead, and there was nothing keeping her this side of that line but the word of a made thing.

"No fine and fancy words now, is it?" Maulhands pressed. "No protestations of innocence, *Oh, sir, I'm only doing puppet shows, no thief I*?" Again that laugh from the others, though Maulhands himself was getting less and less amused, because she was not rising to it. "You thought you'd try your hand at the real world, did you? You apprentice yourself to the Barrio filth, and you're surprised you end up here with the vermin."

"They're better than you."

Maulhands's eyes went wide, because now he had defiance from her but he didn't know what to do with it. For her part, Coppelia had her hands over her mouth even though the words were flown. But she found she meant them, even though they likely weren't true. Doublet had been a literal monster, after all. Rosso was a mean, drunken thug and Auntie had made a living out of threats and blackmail. And yet she stood up and looked Maulhands right in the eye and said, "Stealing's more honest than what you do, Catchpole Lucas, and the only difference between them and your grand masters is that true thieves own to the name."

She wanted the explosion of fury, to goad him just as he'd gone at her. For a moment, he was flushing red, but then he remembered their respective circumstances and an almost sunny expression came to him.

"Good, then," he told her, as though they'd just settled the particulars of a contract between them. "Keach, go fetch the key. Moppet doesn't need her fingers to swing from a rope, and it's not as though she'd be making any more dolls."

Coppelia felt the fear clutch at her, but she had no room left for it. Maulhands would open the door, and then she might as well just launch herself at him, tooth and nail, because apparently this was the worst after all, so what was there to lose?

Except there was no sound of Belly Keach sloping off at Maulhands's order, nor even that rubbery laughter of his. Maulhands glanced about angrily, and then his face drained—paler even in that pale light—and he stepped back from the hatch. In his place, that small square of corridor went on to host the perfect gleaming features of the golem.

There was a lot of stammering and broken excuses from Maulhands, but some unseen gesture of the automaton silenced him. Instead, the creature said, "Bring her," its tones musical, so that she pictured organ pipes and glass chimes within its chest and throat. In seconds, she was out of the cell, standing between Maulhands and his men, following the golem back down to the workshop.

And there it turned to the Broadcaps and ordered them away, and Maulhands's face went purple a bit, but he went, not a word of argument.

She had already looked for the grate, because although she dearly wanted to learn about this gleaming construct, she wanted more to be free. It was back in place and secured by a full half dozen locks and a magic aura, though. No way out but through that richly appointed bedroom and into the cellars of the Siderea palace.

The golem regarded her impassively, and she saw that impassive was its default: its features were lovingly worked to appear as perfectly human as possible, meaning it lacked all those interlocking parts that made Tef or Arc look so anatomised. No frown would ever darken its silver brow, no smile pull up the ruby corners of its lips. The silent regard weighed and weighed on her, but at last, just as she was about to speak, it lifted one leg to plant a boot on a small stool there and stared at her expectantly. The pose was weirdly inappropriate, as though it was a mummer about to slap its thigh and make some ribald remark, but then she remembered who she was and what her skills were, for there, on the black lacquer of its boot, was the scratch from where it had kicked the grate.

A quick glance showed her the tools and materials were all at hand, and it was work well within her mundane skills, let alone her magical gifts. True, she felt a stab of rebellion as she knelt before the creature, but it was subsumed in her professional interest. Here it was, the impossible creation that commanded Broadcaps and magi alike, and apparently, she *was* fit to touch its boot after all.

She worked in silence for a while, and never a bootblack had such an obligingly still customer. At last, though, her curiosity dodged its warders and forced her to say, "Who was it that made you, your honour?" Mimicking Auntie's term of address, for all it hadn't saved the old woman.

She hadn't necessarily expected a reply, but its pleasant, slightly artificial voice tolled back, "Made me? *I* made me, Moppet. That is what they call you, is it not?"

She nodded, keeping her eyes on the boot, using charms to help the new lacquer dry to a pristine shine.

"You don't understand who I am." It sounded as though it wanted to sound disappointed, but there was no room in that beautiful voice for such an emotion.

"The work of some great magus," she hazarded. "One the lesser magicians all respect."

It laughed. The sound almost had her marring her work because it was not something that voice had been intended to do: not a light chuckle but a harsh sound like broken gears, the only ugly thing about it. "Fear, more than respect, but you're right. I made me, and I am that magus, and I am all of this place, and have been since before all living memory."

Arcantel? she thought, though the golem in no way resembled the statue of the great old magus that she knew. Before she could commit her error to words, though, the golem was on with singing its own praises.

"You know my name," it told her. "I am the Archmagister, Shorj Phenrir."

For a moment, she couldn't quite understand the words: she knew them individually, up to and including the name of the chief magus of Loretz, but together and in context, they made no sense. How could this made thing be the Archmagister? A toy or pet of his, surely, or did it mean it was his mouthpiece or herald, through which the ancient mage-lord made his pronouncements?

"He made you . . . ?" She knew she was not following.

"I made me. I became me. I had this body fashioned, the work of a hundred artisans across a decade, each piece made to my exacting requirements, none of them knowing what grand work they were contributing to. For I was old, girlchild. Old already, despite all magic could do. Time is the enemy even magi cannot defeat, they say. I proved them wrong that day. Even as my mortal husk was crumbling, I stabbed the sharpness of my mind into this shell and there I lodged, eternal and unchanging." Its voice strove for triumph, defeated by its own melodious nature, then again by that hideous crunching laugh.

Not that she hadn't been listening, of course, but its little self-congratulatory piece of patter had given her the chance to collect her thoughts. As to the actual revelation, that Phenrir had, in times past, transmuted his consciousness into a construct and become this unliving thing, that was something she stowed to think on later. Right now, she was alone with the most powerful entity in Loretz and apparently permitted to speak, so:

"Master, great lord, your honour . . ." And after larding the sentence with all that, nothing for it but just to ask,

"Why am I here? You cannot lack for artisans to keep your body in shine."

It leant forwards, the jointed ankle of its boot angling to balance its weight. When she looked up, its magnificent visage was right there, not eighteen inches from her own face, eyes like twin fires.

"That is the question, is it not?" it breathed softly. "After all, the workhouses are full of half-magi. When I require repair or restoration, I simply have them brought to me. Why trust my substance to a criminal, for all I see you have performed a workmanlike job."

I have performed a perfect job. A stab of professional annoyance, but she didn't say it. Better to let the thing's metal tongue run on. And of course, there was more pressing material to think and grieve over, hidden in its words, but she had to keep herself focused on her freedom and future, or else she might have neither.

"Your little toys," the golem Phenrir told her. "Don't think I didn't see them. These eyes miss nothing of man or magic. Your little mannikins, that you were so concerned about."

"Toys, great one. Only toys," she croaked out, and then it took the scruff of her neck between cold thumb and forefinger, so precise that it told her, in that gentle but inescapable pinch, of all the untold power its metal digits could apply. She had seen it destroy Rosso's hand, and now she felt how that metal strength was backed by an inhuman control.

"Let us not start off our relationship with lies. I am eternal, Moppet-child. I am truth, and lies are ephemeral. I will not have them in my presence."

She looked up then, though only because its grip permitted. The golem's face was still close, still blithely disconnected from its words and actions. Within the metal she could see the channels of its power, the wealth of bound magic that gave it life.

"Great one, forgive me. My life is spent amongst thieves. Lies are a hard habit, they come so easily. I'm sorry, your honour, sorry—"

It shook her between that thumb-and-finger pinch, ever so slightly, but she felt that it accepted her words, too. After all, if it was Phenrir, then it was one of the mighty, and the mighty loved telling each other how vile the lowly truly were.

And even then, she wondered: about the golem and Phenrir, about the patterns of the magic and just what lies might escape that golden gaze. And it struck her that a hundred mage-lords had come face-to-face with their leader's metal visage over the years, but none of them had her experience of the inanimate animated.

And then it shook her again, less patiently, and she knew she was going to lie anyway, but she would need to season those lies with enough true salt that they would make good eating. She would need to cook those lies to exactly suit the palate of a mage-lord who had lived all his life surrounded by his power and his peers.

9.

SHABBY LILITH YARNEY had never been prone to introspection, but recent events had given her a lot to think on.

The streets of the Barrio were quiet, not just in the late Iron End's parish but everywhere this side of the river. Probably in the Siderea, they were throwing a party about now. The mage-lords had finally set down the law as it applied to the great and to the lowly.

Life in the Barrio was always about tweaking the noses of the rich. For people like Shabby, simply existing, breathing air and taking up space in Loretz was an encroachment on the rights of the worthy and the law-abiding. Plying her actual trade was another affront, flicking the balls of the wealthy as she crept from the slums to steal their stuff. And they egged each other on, the young blades of the Barrio. They grew bold on a diet of each other's regard and envy, until the gutters produced something like Shabby Lilith Yarney, who could slip unremarked into a rich merchant's house, steal his magic boots and his purse of coin and his powdered wig from off his bald head, and leave the Broadcaps wringing their hands and chasing their own shadows. And still the mage-lords had not cared, not even when she started to look into the Siderea itself, where the real money was. The Broadcaps and their half-mage tricks couldn't catch her. The city was her buffet and she ate what she wanted. And when she and Rosso had found a door into the actual palace, then why not pluck the very rings from Shorj Phenrir's fingers while she was at it?

Now she knew why. Now she sat alone in a shadowy booth at the Bag of Teeth and stared at the bottle of wine that would never be enough to drown her sorrows. It wasn't that Rosso was dead, though he and she had lived nine lives together, as the saying went, over their varied and breakneck careers. It wasn't that Gaston Ferrulio was dead, because he wouldn't have shed two tears for her, and she could only manage half a tear for him. It was the harsh reality of it: that she had gone too far and made certain assumptions about her place in the world, and the world had slapped her back hard enough to get forty-nine other people killed. The mage-lords had finally been provoked, and their reaction had been . . . what? Not to flood the streets with Broadcaps, not to hire bounty hunters or conjure demons to track down the malefactors. Just to reach out and crush, like a child with a beetle. A single discharge of their power to incinerate the Iron End and everyone under his roof. A message to Shabby Lilith that all her life to that point had escaped their monstrous justice not because she was fleet or skilled or daring, but because nothing she'd done before had *mattered* enough to them. And now it had, and their response hadn't even caught her, just everyone else.

Draining the bottle, waving for another, she swung wildly between grief and rage. One moment, she was facing a life where she would never dare touch a rich man's coin for fear of crossing that line again and bringing down the lightning on herself and those around her. The next, she seethed with supremely impotent fury that those wastrel magicians had such strength and used it so heedlessly. When had they ever known hunger? When cold, when misery, and yet when the least mote of their authority was questioned, they lashed out like peevish infants! She would go to their places and rob them blind, every one of them, take their inscribed rings and their staves of power, take that gods-damned golem piece by piece if she could. She would make them pay!

Except of course she couldn't, and men and women like that never paid for anything. All of life was a gift to them, and they were too jaded to appreciate it.

The next bottle arrived and she dug the cork out with a stiletto, heedless of crumbs falling down the neck. She was drunk, but it didn't seem like she could ever be drunk enough to get a leash on the way she felt right then.

Taking a deep gulp of the stuff—the worst red rotgut, but she'd never had the Barrioni's sophisticated taste—she slammed the bottle down and slumped back in her seat, glowering out at the gloomy interior of the Bag of Teeth. A good crowd in tonight; any other time, there'd have been singing, gambling, fights. Right now, everyone was weirdly hushed, the murmur of conversation funereal. Everyone had felt the slap when the magi struck. Everyone had read that implicit message: *Know your place.*

There was a tiny little ringing sound, three musical taps against the wine bottle. She glowered, looking up for whoever was gauche enough to disturb her brooding. There was nobody. She heard the sound again, like someone rapping the glass with the handle of a spoon, the pitch of the notes telling her precisely how much she'd already necked. Something moved on the table—she thought it was a rat at first, which to her was a fonder experience than most because in the Barrio, the dogs tended to be fierce and the cats tended to be lunch, and so rats were a good pet for a young girl. Not a rat, though. Something stood on two legs beside the bottle, and plainly she'd drunk more—or worse—than she'd thought, because it looked like a little man. A little metal man, wearing a filmy robe and with a sword slanting over his shoulder—no, not a sword but a cutthroat razor. Shabby goggled at this prodigy, at least half-convinced that it existed only in her head.

It swaggered—genuinely swaggered—out of the wine bottle's shadow, and abruptly she thought of the golem. This miniature was nothing like that polished perfection, but perhaps the mage-lords' revenge wasn't over yet. Perhaps they had sent out this *thing* to cut her throat. . . .

She stood suddenly, jarring the table with her knee, upsetting the bottle. The metal man fell into a crouch, riding the motion, not even dropping his weapon. At the same time, something landed on her shoulder and a crisp voice whispered in her ear, "Easy, now. Sit back down, if you please."

Shabby froze, staring out at the taproom, much of which was staring back at her. They couldn't see what was on the table, she knew. They couldn't see what was on her shoulder. And if there was another razor at the service of that little voice, then things were about to go very badly for her. Her wine-sodden mind tried to think through the fug to get to some kind of plan, the sort of derring-do she was famed for. Instead, she just sat down as she was bid, her inspiration apparently fully soluble in alcohol.

"My friend wanted to be the one on your shoulder. But we want to talk, and I thought having a blade at your throat wouldn't be conducive," said that damnable voice.

Shabby found one of her hands moving ever so gently, finding the bottle's neck and righting it, for all the contents were mostly soaking into the sawdust of the floor. And there her hand remained, because she reckoned that she could bring the base down on that metal man hard enough, and worry about the devil on her left shoulder after.

"So, the mage-lords have a message for me, do they?" she asked, as lightly as she could.

"What?" the voice demanded, and the metal man on the table adopted an exaggerated pose of incredulous outrage.

"We're no work of theirs," the unseen shoulder-rider said. "We're the Moppet's."

Shabby took a moment to process what that meant, and her grip on the bottle loosened. "You were there?"

"We were there." A scratch and a scuttle and something spidered down her arm to the table: a doll of wood, marvellously made and moving under its own power. Its face was a jigsaw of tiny features arrayed into a bold and challenging expression Shabby had seen in the mirror more than once. "And Moppet's still there," the wooden figure called up to her. "And we're going to get her back. And we want you to help."

～

Doctor Losef had an elixir guaranteed to banish drunkenness and abolish hangovers, though Shabby had to virtually kick his door down to get him to sell it to her, because he hadn't opened shop like usual. She found the froglike man sitting in his vest in the backroom where he slept and lived and did everything not actually involving perpetrating alchemy or selling it to people. His pop-eyed look to her was mournful.

"Sharp cider, Sweaty," she told him.

For a long moment, he just stared at her solemnly, a face like some toad-cult's Masque of Tragedy, but at last he stirred himself.

"Already with the schemes, Shabby?" he asked her. "Put it all behind you?"

"That I have not," she told him. She swiped the proffered mug from him and drained it down to its tin bottom. The liquid tasted so vile that it routed all the drunk from her mind in an instant. The aftertaste was even worse.

"The Broadcaps are all over Sallow Chapel Parish," Losef told her. "You know, Cup-Eater's turf. Broke into three dens and the Royal Spoon and took away nineteen of the Barrio's finest. Nobody raised a finger. They'd be doing it here if they didn't think we were already beat. Everyone sees the smoke and thinks, *Look at 'em funny, could be us next.*"

Shabby shook her head, the sharp cider making her feel very sharp indeed. Energy was thrumming through her limbs and crackling from her fingers. "So, it would be a right fool who went and pulled the Archmagister's nose about now, wouldn't it?"

Losef regarded her. "So, so foolish."

For a moment, the pair of them just looked at each other, trying to gauge mood without asking anything incriminating. Then Shabby sniffed the air and stuck her head through the doorway to Losef's laboratory. "Big old cauldron on the boil there, Sweaty," she noted. "Smells like someone's cooking up an extra-large batch of Doctor Losef's Famous Quick-Acting Laxative."

Losef coughed. "It might be," he said quietly, "that someone has a kitchen hand at the Broadcap barracks owes them a big favour. It might be that someone is very, very angry, despite his seemingly mellow disposition, and intends to take what petty revenge he can." And on that word, *revenge,* she heard the spine in him, the iron buried down there beneath the greasy skin and saggy fat.

And then he said, "But perhaps you are about a piece of more worthy daring. It would be just like you." And she felt such an absurd surge of affection for the misbegotten alchemist, because he had faith in her, which was more than she herself did.

"Back room of the Bag of Teeth, tonight," she told him.

"Bring your best tricks. And some of the Quick-Acting. Who knows."

~

And he came, complete with bandolier and pack, laden with vials and flasks all carefully wrapped and labelled in his own alchemist's argot. He came to find Shabby back in her finest second-storey gear, all her magical trinkets out of hock or storage, reclaimed from borrowers, stolen back from fellow thieves. Gloves, bandana, brooch of shadow, belt of chains, little pieces of Barrio mythology drained to the last crusts of their power and trotted out now one more time.

She was already playing host to a big, long-boned man whom Losef plainly hadn't looked for. "You're supposed to be dead," he pointed out.

Kernel Jointmaker, chief enforcer of the late lamented Iron End, looked murder at him, but right now, that was his standard expression for anything that his gaze fell on. He had always been the mongrel hound in Ferrulio's court, the rough edge that overambitious rogues sometimes cut themselves on. Right now, he looked as though only an extreme act of will was keeping him from a butchering spree from there all the way to the Siderea.

He'd been out on errands, he'd told Shabby. Which

meant breaking legs to Ferrulio's order. And so, he'd not been there when his lord and master, and the entire structure he'd given his life to, was obliterated by one errant exercise of power. He'd come to seek her out, though, and she thought he'd probably pitched up with the intention of making her a few new joints to punish her for surviving. Thankfully, of course, she'd had a better use of his gifts to propose.

"So, the three of us, is it?" Losef asked. "Against the Convocation?"

"Not just the three of us," Shabby said, steepling her fingers and making the enchanted embroidery of her gloves dance. "Got a few new tricks, just, you know, little things that might help."

10.

THE HAND HAD COME surprisingly quickly. But then Coppelia was used to working on a far finer scale, and she had the very best tools. Tools she could never have dreamt of, not long before. The finest manufacture, imbued with the most elegant enchantments, each one the work of mage-artisans of surpassing skill. They caught any of her own slips and flaws and gave her the time and chance to avoid them; they let her work metal as though it was the wood she was more used to, magnified her half-magery, allowing her to perform the feats of a master, to reach a potential that her own poor tinker's kit back in the Barrio could never have permitted. Part of her exalted, despite everything, that she might create anything as wonderful as this, even if nobody ever knew, even if she died alone here the moment she was done. She had not thought, in truth, that she had the soul of a crafter, but now it stirred in her, wings beating with pride.

And while she worked, she could put aside all the other thoughts that were trying to invade her mind, the thoughts that had nothing to do with pride and accomplishment and everything to do with grief and horror and hate. But the moment she paused—finished at the lathe or the drill, letting a part dry, returning to the yellowing schematics she had been given—they all came flocking back. She would stop, dead still, in that underground workshop, fists clenching as she did battle with the furies inside her that cried for revenge, for justice. But she was a thief, and what did she know of justice? Save that it was a lip-service word for the mighty to enforce their will on her.

Auntie Countless was dead. Coppelia had known her for years. The old woman had been a rogue and probably some kind of spy once upon a time, but she had been kind to the Moppet, an aunt in all but blood. Coppelia thought of her bitter tea, her shelves of mismatched ornaments, the way she had carved a unique little niche in the world of the Barrio. And now a Broadcap's thuggish stroke had broken her head, here in this very room. Were it not for the mindless enchantments that tidied and cleaned the place every evening, the stain would still be on the floor.

And the others were probably dead, too. Perhaps the homunculi had escaped, but probably Shabby and Losef had been hunted down. Doublet had been half-obliterated, and she knew they had tortured Rosso before they hanged him, to find who put them up to the heist. She knew because Lucas Maulhands had told her, in that way of his that was gloating pretending it was righteousness. She hated him more than she hated Phenrir, really. Phenrir was inhuman, after all—not just that he inhabited a metal body, but that he was one of the Convocation whose temporal and magical power seemed to place them beyond any human empathy or connection. Maulhands was just a man, and he couldn't even gloat honestly. He must dress his every action with the stiff cloth of law and proper conduct, unable to own up to the fact that he was as much of a mean bastard as any of the criminals he chased.

And now she was assembling the thumb. She had improved on the schematics, adding more motion to the joints to give the golem a greater freedom of movement. Possibly, that would get her killed because it wasn't what she had been asked for. Craftsmanship had prodded her, initially: whoever drew up the plans had probably not been told the purpose for their work. They had produced something that might suit an automaton or music-box dancer, capable of certain elegant motions but not the full living range of human digits. She had found herself modifying the plan right from the outset, and all those wonderful tools and lenses had shown her how to accomplish everything she set her mind to. But then her mind had run on to self-preservation, because there had been many other artisans kept down here, to work and rework the golem's metal frame, and they were not here now. No imagination was required to understand what had happened to them when their continued presence had been unnecessary. If she could show herself as something more than a mere replacer and maintainer, she could extend the period of her usefulness and thus her life. She would keep out of Maulhands's wringing grasp a month longer, maybe more.

And later had come that other thought, that led her to scrap some work and redo it, going ever further from the plan, because rebellion could not be kept down in her for long, and a slightly longer life was not, alone, enough. She would *know* the truth before she died, even if the only thing she could do with it was take it to her unmarked grave.

She went back to the plans—now annotated freely in her own hand, that was cramped and ran the words together because, back home, scraps of paper were a precious commodity. Time to join the two articulated sections of thumb to the rod extending into the hand itself, but before she could submerge herself in the work once more, another wave of grief struck her. Not Auntie, this time, though that fire still burned hot. The dream that Auntie had, all innocently, given her, though. The thing that had fired her to come there in the first place, beyond any need of the homunculi.

And she could not know, honestly, whether it was this that her parents had been taken for. There must be other mage-lords beyond Phenrir who had tasks they needed skilled mage-artisans for, whose labour went on behind closed doors, and whose silence was bought with a knife or a flash of magic when the work was done. She knew full well that plenty of people disappeared from the workhouses who were skilled at their trades and who were painted with the brush of some wrongdoing or other to excuse their absence. But some of them came there, and her parents had been of her trade, had taught her much of what she knew before they all arrived in this damned city, seeking opportunity. And when Phenrir came hunting promising candidates to polish and maintain his metal parts, it seemed inescapable that he would have looked down the lists and seen those names. And so she decided it was true, because even a little certainty, even certainty that was entirely self-crafted, was better than that great fug of not knowing. Her parents had been brought here. They had puzzled over these plans, or others from the same shelf. They had corrected the set of Phenrir's gleaming nose or oiled the motion of his knee. They had repaired the fine filigree of the coat he wore, that was a part of him and moved like cloth even though it was fine-linked mail. Like her, perhaps they had knelt before him as they polished his boots.

Her fingernails had left white crescents in her palms when she mastered herself again. She fought down the impulse to take one of her little whitesmith's hammers or the crank handle for the big vice and lash it at Phenrir's perfect metal face when he appeared. She knew it would feel fine, in that instant, to cause more ducatti of damage in a single second than she could ever have honestly earned in a lifetime. But most likely, Phenrir would catch her with his remaining hand before she even landed the blow, and then he would crush her wrist just like he had done with Rosso, and she would die soon after, but worse than that, she would never *know*. Because she had a thought, based on her own examination of the golem and her unique experience. She had a hypothesis she wished to test before the end.

~

In the end, the lie she had told him had been as finely crafted as any part of his body, a masterwork fabrication fit to be placed on a pedestal and taught to apprentice dissemblers for generations to come.

"The little people," he had demanded. "Who made them? How were they here? They were not just automata. I could see the magic in them." Most likely because he saw the same patterns in the mirror.

Knee-jerk, then, to say they were hers, that she built them, but that lie would out far too swiftly if he set her to duplicate the feat. And it would not give her space and time without the golem's burning gaze hanging over her shoulder, either. She needed to thread a needle whereby she was interesting enough to keep alive but where he had other demands on his valuable time.

"They came to me," she had said. "In the Barrio. Because of my craftsmanship. Their master sent them to negotiate for my services. It was through them all this business came about. It was to their order that the thieves gathered, to come to your workshop." All lies, but seasoned with just the right amount of truth.

The golem had taken her chin between thumb and forefinger, hard enough to leave twin bruises; hard enough to just hint at the crushing power there that could cave in her jaw any time it wanted. "Who was their master?" it demanded.

She gagged about that grip until it relented and let her speak, and then gabbled out that she didn't know, not for sure (because it was only good thiefcraft that such a patron would act through intermediaries, and surely the golem would guess that). Even as it reached for her again, though, she babbled that Shabby had managed to trail the little things a ways, because the same question had been on the thieves' minds, too.

"To the Siderea," she said. "They went up the wall. And we knew it must be one of the Convocation who sent them, for who else might enchant such wonders?" The workshops of her mind were minting sincerity in unprecedented quantities, depressing the market for years to come with their adulterated coinage. "Not knowing it was your workshop, Archmagister, we thought perhaps they came from *you*." And with just enough starry-eyed awe, the gutter urchin confronted the magnificence of Loretz's master-mage, because if the mighty craved one thing, it was validation, knowing in their heart of hearts that they were never so grand as they styled themselves; even when they were made of gold and gems.

And that had been enough; the bejeweled fish was hooked. She had seen the other magi when they had come with their Broadcaps. She had read their expressions, she whose work was to fabricate the human face and its character. She had seen their sneers and their schadenfreude at their leader being discomfited, even as they had set their thugs on the thieves. There was neither love nor trust amongst the Convocation: united against their lessers but divided against each other. Of all the stories she could possibly have told to Shorj Phenrir, none would have been so readily believed as that one of his own close confidantes was behind the outrage. Not even the truth.

And the homunculi were safe, at least for now. Nobody would come hunting them above Coppelia's studio while Phenrir was trying to determine which of his underlings needed slapping down.

~

When he came back to her, she had no idea if he had settled on a target or not. It wasn't something he was likely to discuss with her, after all. Instead, she just presented the finished hand for his approval, devoid of scratches, lovingly cleansed of Rosso's blood and with improvements made to the joints. Now would be the test, in more ways than one. The test of her theory; the test of whether her alterations would merit punishment for deviating from his strict instructions.

Reattaching the hand to Phenrir's wrist was an education in itself. She had never thought much about how the homunculi themselves might deal with injury or damage. She knew they wore out—each with a lifespan dictated by experience and the robustness of its construction. If Arc lost a foot, though, could they smith him a new one and join it to him? She hadn't thought so, from snippets of conversation between him and Tef. Injury was as real to them as to her. Except now she knew it could be done.

There were certain innovations set down in the schematics that channelled and shaped the flow of magic, letting it reach out minutely from any incomplete edge of Phenrir's body, greedy to regain perfection. She could see it flickering at his wrist as though some insect lurked there, its antennae reaching cautiously out into the air. When she brought the hand near, the magic stretched, filings to a magnet, dancing about the joints of the wrist as she slotted in the pins and carefully tightened the screws that held him together. Before her mage-sight, the magic advanced through the restored hand, joint to joint, cautiously, like Broadcaps searching a house. She held her breath as they reached the thumb, where her modifications had been greatest, but her work passed muster and the magic made a home there as readily as in the rest.

It flexed each finger, and she could picture so clearly every joint and bevel of it, the interplay of sections sliding past one another, oiled and clean. There was nothing to be read in its stern features, but of course there never could be. Slowly, Shorj Phenrir's golem brought the refurbished hand up to its burnished gaze. *And does it see, truly, with those orbs?* She thought it probably did, even though it shouldn't need to. The magic could have taken in the outside world from anywhere about its body, but it had been made by human hands, limited by human minds. *How does it work for Tef and Arc? I must ask.* And then the bleak understanding that she'd never have the opportunity.

"What have you done?" Not angry, not yet. It moved each finger, each one with a little more freedom, more sideways play, better rotation at the base, more like a human hand. And then the thumb. She watched the digit hook inwards, then fold back, and further back, reclining smoothly until it was flat alongside the line of the golem's arm, inhumanly so. Phenrir made a sound, and it was not shocked or angry or even squeamish to see its own hand twisted so, but only thoughtful.

"I thought," Coppelia said with a tremble in her voice she didn't have to feign, "that I could do better. Your plans were for a puppet. Not . . ." *Whatever you really are.* But she turned the thought into a gesture she hoped looked admiring.

"It is good." It brought up its other hand, flexing the thumb through its limited, human arcs of motion. "You will do the same with the other. And the fingers also?" And the slight question there made her heart leap because it implied a need to ask. It implied that she had been promoted from disposable resource to something permitted to answer, even if that answer absolutely had to be *yes.*

"I would be honoured to work on you," she told it, and that was not entirely a lie. And then she carefully disassembled its wrist joint so she could have the other hand for modification, the tradecraft part of her mind already thinking about how she could make it better.

"I will have food sent," it told her. "Work well, and there will be better food, and other things you may wish."

She bowed and made all the right grateful noises. "And perhaps there might be other parts I could improve, Archmagister. I was wondering . . . your face is fine, but I could make it move: eyebrows, lips."

"Perhaps." But plainly, such fripperies were not as important to it. She had seen with Rosso how it valued being able to get its hands dirty from time to time.

And then it left her to the workshop, its right hand lying shorn of life and magic on the bench, and she wondered if she was right, and just what it was that looked out from that metal skull.

11.

THEY WOULDN'T JUST BE walking in through the front gates this time, and nobody much fancied trying the same underground access as before. An alerted Convocation had the wherewithal to put far more dangerous obstacles down there than just a few sewer predators or noxious air. And besides, they had no Auntie or Moppet to coddle, or Doublet, who had never been one for the more energetic feats of larceny. Shabby had been scaling walls as soon as she'd been toddling, and with her gloves, she could go up them like a lizard. Kernel Jointmaker's long limbs were made for climbing as well as his hands were for strangling, and Sweaty Losef had an unguent for his fingers and toes that let him gum his way up slowly but surely. Shabby let each in turn borrow her cloak, that turned away any mundane eyes that might glance their way from the city below. Up top, if there was a scrying in place that would alert the mage-lords, well, that was beyond their control. The wall was long, though, and she reckoned they were too tight-fisted with their power to spend it so profligately. Besides, she reckoned they wouldn't expect anything quite so mad as a second invasion from the Barrio. The den of rogues was well and truly slapped down, they'd think, what with the explosive end of Gaston Ferrulio.

On the wall top, they were nearly discovered. A Broadcap was walking that windswept beat, bundled in his cloak against night's early chill. Kernel was all for stuffing any alarm back down the man's throat with the point of a knife, but they didn't know how long their sojourn in the Siderea was going to be, and a found body and a missing man would both attract attention. She tried the cloak, casting it over the three of them in the hope the bored sentry would just amble past. Close on, he stopped, though—likely he was a bit of a half-mage himself and his magical senses were tweaking at him, telling him something was wrong.

Before Kernel could take matters into his own bloody hands, Sweaty popped up. From the Broadcap's expression he must have been a sight, a froggy-looking man leaping out of nowhere like a puppet devil in a morality play. He dashed a phial full of liquid right in the man's face just as the sentry tried to call for help, and a moment later, the Broadcap was on his knees, then on his face.

They propped him up, and before Kernel could get down to the knife work he was so plainly up for, Losef took out a flask and doused the man's face and the front of his robe. At Shabby's look, the alchemist smiled weakly.

"No great tradecraft, this, just some good rum I will miss later. But this is a lonely watch; small wonder this fellow decided to knock off for a drink or five. And the rest was my Patent Insomnia Cure and he won't remember a blessed thing that happened to him since three this afternoon, at that concentration."

"You don't like killing, do you?" Kernel accused him, as though this was the worst failing imaginable.

"I don't like many things," Sweaty Losef replied mildly. "Some of them are, sadly, unavoidable."

The other side of the wall was designed to be descended from, with grand steps every few hundred yards for when the great and the good wanted to go up for a bit of lording it over all they surveyed. Getting to the rich pickings of the Siderea was no great trick, then, but Sweaty and Jointmaker were both keen to know how she was going to effect entry into the palace, and Shabby remained close-mouthed about it, just in case it failed her. Oh, she had backup plans, in case the trick she had literally up her sleeve turned out to be worthless, but her curiosity was hooked. She wanted to see if it would work.

The palace had many doors, but only a few familiar to the Convocation. The thieves weren't going anywhere near those, for obvious reasons. However, even mage-lords needed to eat, and their servants and menials had to go in and out through mean little gates tucked out of sight of their masters so as not to spoil the view. Oh, there were windows up above, of course, where an energetic burglar could gain access, but that was where the mage-lords kept their chambers. They never slept, nor did their lanterns dim—even now, there was the sound of music and laughter rolling out into the night. None of Shabby's shabby little crew would pass for magi, nor even for their menials. And though Shabby had a particular guilty fondness for those tatty romances where a young girl from the Barrio steals into the palace, to be discovered by a handsome magus who merely winks at her and lets her about her business (to lead to later assignation, the elevation of the girl's place in society, and the shock discovery that she was some lost scion of a well-born family all this time!), she wasn't such a fool as to believe in them.

But here was a tradesman's entrance, under the shadow of a balcony where the great and the good were carousing and talking about one another's sartorial failings. The thieves had made it through a garden unobserved, with Shabby and Losef working overtime to avoid those parts of the greenery enchanted to snare those without an invitation.

"You're saying they don't lock them?" Kernel asked.

"Locked, certainly," Shabby confirmed.

He crouched, staring at the gilded wood, even this meagre portal adorned with as much ornament as his late master's fondest possessions. "Magicked, too, then?"

"Of course. Just be patient."

Easy enough to say that to him, but she was feeling twitchy herself. One pair of magi had already swanned past in the dark, off for a liaison in the arbour. On the upside of the ledger, that suggested the Broadcaps didn't patrol there, but Shabby still felt taut as a viol string. She'd lost that extra weight from her sleeves a little while ago, and she could only hope that the little things she was relying on would fall out as she hoped.

"I have some acids . . ." Sweaty started, but then there was a shimmer from the door that froze them all in place, waiting to see if it was the prelude to discovery. In the next breath, the door sagged in its frame, not from the lock side but off its hinges, so that Kernel lunged forwards to catch it before it fell on the three of them.

"Subtle," he complained, and Shabby was privately agreeing, but for his eyes she just shrugged and gestured as if to say, *Well, we're in, aren't we?*

She felt a tug at her collar, a little form scurrying up her cloak hem like a rat and nestling in her thrown-back cowl.

"Seriously?" she murmured.

"Couldn't do the lock," Tef's scratchy voice came in her ear. "Nobody wards the hinges, though."

Doctor Losef had some adhesive that sufficed to put the door back in place after they'd crossed inside, though if anyone came to try the handle, the whole business would fall on them. Still, the mage-lords probably weren't expecting any deliveries until the small hours, and Shabby dearly hoped they'd be long gone by then.

～

Tef rode Shabby's shoulder for a while, because the woman had bought a map of the palace downstairs from some poor human who'd been a maidservant for the mage-lords before she'd grown too old for their eyes to find pleasing, and who'd then descended by misstep and misfortune to end up in the Barrio. Tef was only just beginning to understand what the Barrio was and what the Siderea was, and all the parishes in between, but she already felt a curious loyalty to the gutters. Nowhere in this city was her place, but the Barrio was for those who had no other place, so it was hers as well.

They were able to dodge the servants and a pair of idling Broadcaps, all the way to where stone stairs spiralled down into the earth. There were cellars of enchanted wine down there, vaults, laboratories, abandoned storerooms. And, somewhere, there was that opulent buried bedchamber and its workshop.

That, Tef knew, was where their interests were likely to diverge. Shabby knew the homunculi were there to rescue Moppet, and the thief plainly wasn't averse to that happening, with that tenuous loyalty the Barrioi showed one another. Revenge against the magi was the grander aim for the three humans, though. Revenge for their lost comrades, their dead leader; revenge for lifetimes beneath the boot-heel. In their incendiary reprisal, the Convocation had pushed these three villains just too far. They were here to pillage, and perhaps to kill.

"Where now?" Shabby whispered, the three rogues hiding in the shadow of the wine casks.

"Wait here," Tef told her, and hopped down to rejoin the others.

Shallis had stayed back at the colony, of course. Her magic would have been useful, but she was fragile and, besides, disapproved of the whole venture, though not enough to forbid it. Her authority was dissolving into an on-the-fly democracy where everyone had a fair say, and perhaps she was glad to shed the responsibility. Kyne and Lief had stayed back, too, with Lief's new child Lori. As well as parental duties, he was the best crafter amongst them, and Kyne the Fabricker was their raven-handler. If all else went wrong, those four could keep the colony alive.

But the others were all there, some under protest. Tef and Arc, obviously, but Effl Ratkiller had refused to be left behind, and she was quick and fierce as her name suggested. Then there was Morpo the Candling, who was neither, but who was a better magus than Tef or any of them save Shallis herself. Morpo emphatically did not want to be there, but they needed him, and just as his wax body was mutable and soft, so was he.

Tef reached the other three homunculi, who were out across the great expanse of the cellar floor. Arc had his razor over one shoulder, but the others bore a new burden: the articulated hand that Moppet had made, which was too large for any sensible purpose.

"Have you puppets worked out where we're headed yet?" she demanded. *Puppet* had become something of a fashionable insult between them recently.

"Yes," Morpo said sullenly, and "No," said the other two, so that Tef felt like cuffing them all but at last turned to the sagging features of the Candling.

"What, now?"

"Here." Morpo took the outsize hand off Arc and traced designs on its palm so that the wooden fingers trembled and flexed. A moment later, the hand jumped to the ground and lay there, one finger extended towards the nearest wall.

"It's broken," Arc said. "Or Morpo is."

"Shut up, rust-head."

"Bee's-leavings."

Tef slapped the pair of them, leaving a dent in Morpo's head and not discomfiting Arc remotely. "Effl, go find what's there. A catch, the line of a door, some moving part."

The mouse-skull head of the scrimshander cocked at her. Effl had added a ratskin cloak to her outlandish look now, with some fly-wings tied to the head of her spear like a pennant. Tef thought she'd argue, but then the Ratkiller was off, bounding across the cellar and scaling a rank of barrels with the frantic speed of a spider. A moment later, she was waving her spear in circles from the top. *Found something.*

"Go help," she told the others, and ran back to the thieves to impart directions to the cavernous space of Shabby's ear.

By the time the humans were over, the homunculi were hidden. Shabby hadn't wanted to trust the others with their existence, not just yet. Effl had helpfully outlined part of the hidden door, leaving scratches in the stone that drew attention to it. The humans puzzled over the mechanism for a short while before it swung open. Tef saw Morpo reforming himself, down in the shadow of the casks; he had oozed his semiliquid body through the crack and found a more obvious lever on the other side. It wasn't a very pleasant trick for him to pull, to hear him tell it, and he cast her a glowering look as she passed.

The human known as Sweaty had his reddish lamps to take them this far, but they reached lit areas soon—globes of cold fire hanging on chains from the ceiling showing that palace residents were abroad there. There were distant voices, too, and the occasional scuff of footsteps, all echoing in such a way that human and homunculus senses were constantly being tweaked and strained.

The four homunculi reached a crossroads, and Arc got out the hand again. Effl had a nub of flint palmed, for the plan was they'd leave arrows for Shabby to see now they were down there, meaning the human could pretend to be finding a path in fact laid out for her. Tef suspected the thief would have been able to find her own way eventually, but the sympathetic bond between Moppet and her creation was speeding them on their path.

"Well, it's mostly pointing down," Morpo observed glumly. "I told you this would happen."

"Only mostly," Arc said. "But a bit that way."

"Then we'll go that way and I'll warn Shabby she might need to double back." They all went still as someone laughed from down the corridor. *Let's hope it's not* that *way.*

"As quickly as we can, too. Go on ahead and take another reading at the next turn."

Effl scaled the wall with her flint and scratched the arrow, even as the humans approached. It was that sound—not their soft talk, not the thieves' soft shoes—that attracted hostile notice.

There had been a human there all along. He had been sitting in an alcove, a monstrous great shadow amongst other shadows, and they had been so intent on their business, they hadn't seen him. That was the problem with humans. They were so big that they just became part of the landscape when they were still.

This wasn't one of the magi, thankfully, but it was one of their servants, with the blue robes and hat, a Broadcap who had probably come down there for an illicit nap and now gawped out, first up at Effl, then forward at the thieves.

Effl went for him, as bold against the towering might of a human as she might be against a rat. The Broadcap had some magic to him, a scrap of it, like so many in this city. He was partway through sounding some alarm or launching some attack when the scrimshander's fishhook spear drove into his face, just below his eye.

The magic fell apart instantly, sheared through by the man's pain. He managed a fragment of a shriek before the biggest human, the Jointmaker, lunged forwards and got a big hand about the Broadcap's mouth, slamming the man's head back into the wall. His other hand punched in three times, fast enough that Tef flinched, because humans were supposed to be slow and ponderous. The third time, there was a knife involved, and that was the end of it.

Jointmaker stepped back, the knife still very much in evidence, and his eyes were on Effl, who had retreated up the wall.

"What the fuck's this?" he hissed.

"Not just that!" came Arc's tinny bellow from the ground, and Jointmaker looked down to find his boot being rapped by the butt of the Scull's razor.

"Remarkable," Sweaty said, though not in any way that suggested he was happy about it.

"They're with me," Shabby told them. "They belong to the Moppet, Auntie's apprentice. She made them." Not true, but as much as any humans needed to know.

"Fuck me," Jointmaker said, staring goggle-eyed down at Arc. For a moment, he might have done anything, most likely something violent. Tef thought about how quick he was, and how a stomp of that boot would turn Arc into nothing more than broken pieces.

"Kernel," Shabby said, warningly.

"What's the world coming to?" the big human said. "I remember when this was simple. And now there's little doll people threatening me with a shave. Fuck me."

"And?"

"And fine. Though Moppet's going to have some questions when . . ." And then something set in his face, like pieces of expression getting stuck halfway, because of course there wasn't anyone to ask those questions, not anymore. "Fine."

"Sweaty?"

"Remarkable," the alchemist human repeated. "Lead on, before this unfortunate is discovered."

"You can't . . . dissolve the body or something? You said you had acids."

"Not a whole bathful of them, alas."

"Then let's go."

~

The business with the Broadcap had been a salutary lesson that the little people were not infallible. Shabby had gotten complacent, she decided. She needed to remember just how much trouble they were all walking into.

The precise form of her revenge was still taking form, but it would involve the workshop. Worse came to worst, she would have Jointmaker's muscle and Sweaty's acids just wreck the place beyond use, a piece of childish vandalism that would nevertheless provide considerable satisfaction.

You kick us, we kick back. Jointmaker wanted to cut some magicianly throats, and possibly that would also be on the menu for the night, but Shabby decided she didn't want to push her luck or dirty her hands quite that much.

What she really wanted was to get the drop on that golem and ruin all that lovely workmanship in the name of teaching it that Rosso, Auntie and Doublet had been worth more than all its jewels and fine enamels. What she wanted was to find a vault of other, more portable treasures in a cupboard off that workshop, that she could spread all over the Barrio at cut-down prices so that half the thieves in the city might find their art enhanced to the detriment of their betters. What she really wanted . . .

In her heart, she knew that what she wanted was to undo absolutely all of it: to reverse Ferrulio's mission, unspeak her own words that set him on the trail, bring back lost friends, forget it ever happened and let us never mention this again to the whole of the last few days. But she reckoned even the Convocation wasn't hiding away anything that smart, so she'd settle on breaking things to show the mage-lords that even she, even Shabby Lilith Yarney, was a human being who couldn't be trampled on without consequence.

They were deeper down now, following the scratch-marks of the homunculi. So far, the little people had led them true, or at least they hadn't had to go back on themselves at all. If it turned out they really were diminutive agents of the Convocation, then everything was already screwed, of course, but the ship of doubting them had well and truly sailed by now.

Even as she thought it, Tef was on her shoulder again. It was a little spooky, how they could just come and go so stealthily; Shabby was already considering just what weal a long-term partnership might bring when all this was over.

"What now?" she asked.

"We're . . . not sure. The hand is crawling around in circles."

"I thought it just pointed?"

"Yes." They were approaching a widening of the ways, a room up ahead. Shabby ducked down to crouch at the doorway, seeing only more of the same. The clutch of Tef's fingers on her earlobe felt like tiny pins.

"So?"

"It means there's magic, active magic. The hand was made to take it in so it could move. Moppet did well there," Tef explained. "But now it's drawing on whatever's around."

"So, what is around? Are we . . . *over* the workshop, maybe?"

"Could be. We'll need to scout around again. I'm sorry."

The room ahead was lopsided, she saw, more to one

side of the passage than the other. *Another hidden door?* As she slipped inside with the others on her heels, she murmured to Tef, "No, it's good. Be sure." A sudden stab of loss: talking to the little made thing as though it were a fellow rogue on a job, like she would talk to Rosso, with infinite faith in his ability to pull off his part of the caper.

She felt the little wooden creature part company with her, signalling for Kernel and Losef to halt. The big bruiser stayed on his feet, scowling about as though annoyed by the lack of warm bodies to turn cold. Sweaty sat down gratefully and took off one shoe to massage his foot.

"Who even needs this many passages?" he demanded plaintively.

"Lots of mage-lords," Jointmaker grunted. "Give one a lab or a safe room or a kinky dungeon, they all want one."

Shabby was about to hush them when the feel of the room changed about her. She had good senses—mundane senses, anyway—and she knew from the way the air met her ears if she was in a narrow place or a grand one, a low or high ceiling. Abruptly, the room was twice the size to her ears, and she whirled round to find that lopsidedness gone, the chamber expanded, or rather the illusory wall whisked away. Revealed were a pair of slightly in-flagrante magicians. There was a man there, and a woman, and the woman's robe was halfway to her waist, the man's part-hitched to his belt. They had plainly been able to see through their side of the wall, though, because neither was looking startled and the man was looking very smug indeed.

"Kinky dungeons," he echoed disdainfully, and Jointmaker went for him without comment, knives out. He got almost precisely halfway before the magus's beringed hands flicked out and froze him in midstep and caught Shabby and Losef as well.

She watched him approach, not even bothering to reshevel his clothing. He was a tall, handsome man, likely not as young as he appeared, but that was magic for you. He had a square jaw touched with a neat and regular fuzz of beard, and Shabby could see the magic glare from every piece of cloth or ornament on him. Certainly, whatever trick he'd pulled had her every muscle locked, nothing moving of her save her breathing and her heartbeat. She couldn't even look sidelong at Sweaty to see if he had anything up his sleeve.

If the magus was about to fall for her lower-class beauty and let her off with a promise of later assignations, there was no more sign of it in his handsome face than there was warmth.

"Lucrece," he said. "I think we've caught some vagabonds."

The woman was also very beautiful, all honey skin and hair like the waters of a dark pool flowing past her shoulders. She tugged her robe up and sent a look at her companion's back that told Shabby a great deal about their respective place in the magical pecking order. It was a tired look that wanted to hate the man it was turned on but knew that she'd have that robe pushed down past her cleavage again soon enough because he had power and position she had to indulge if she wanted to keep her own. Shabby wanted to smile at her; it was a Barrio expression, even here beneath the palace. The magic stopped her doing even that.

"You'd think they'd have learned their lesson," the mage-lord said, standing before Jointmaker. "Perhaps I should have them eat their own tongues or something."

"Firmin, don't," said Lucrece, making a final adjustment to her robe, a twitch of her fingers that magically restored the wide collar's unlikely positioning: bare shoulders and no possible mundane means of support. At her companion's arched eyebrow, and to defend against any accusation of unseemly mercy, she added, "The Archmagister will want to see them."

Firmin looked mulish at that but then shrugged. "I suppose," he agreed. "Let's have them march themselves off to Shorj and show him he can't control his vermin problem. I'd say I can't wait to see his face, but that's hardly appropriate with him, now, is it?"

12.

COPPELIA WAS BACK IN her cell to sleep—whatever détente she'd worked out with Phenrir's golem did not extend to more salubrious quarters. Still, she'd thought she could at least count on an uninterrupted night so she could be sharp for the work in the morning. Instead, at some time that felt like midnight, she was shocked into wakefulness by Lucas Maulhands and his cronies Belly and Lynx storming in and hauling her off the straw mattress.

"What?" she demanded. "What do you want?" Abruptly, she was convinced this was a frolic of their own and they'd decided to give her a good kicking off the record.

"Himself has sent for you" was what Maulhands had to say, though, so apparently, any kickings to be administered would be entirely in the Broadcaps' official capacity. Still, there was a definite personal touch in the way he wrenched her arm as he hauled her out of the cell, a promise that just because it was all law and justice didn't mean he couldn't enjoy it.

"Why?" she exploded. "Why are you even here? Why aren't you in Fountains Parish doing your job, Catchpole? Since when were you a turnkey at the palace?"

He rammed her back against the wall to answer, but she'd been expecting that, welcomed it almost, because it was the way the world worked on sane days, and she was short of those right now.

"I told them I knew you, Moppet," Maulhands ground out. "I told them, she's a tricky one, got a mouth on her, talk you through four sides of a triangle if you let her. So, maybe I ought to keep an eye, eh? Seeing as me and my lads from the parish know her. And after all, you've talked your way out of a whipping or a hanging already, somehow. So, I know you're up to something."

And, just as when he'd told her she was a thief, he wasn't wrong, but she wasn't about to admit anything of the sort. Instead, she had in her that true villain's sense of outrage, that all this *law* could be there making her life difficult.

"Why, Catchpole? Lucas Maulhands, why?" she demanded, suddenly beyond any care about a slap or a boot in the ribs. "Why am I so much your damned business that it's come to this?"

For a moment, he just stared at her, and she tried to interpret his expression. There was a connection between them; that was what this interest of his seemed to say.

Did he harbour some qualms, that he could have kept her on the straight and narrow if he'd only got her back to the orphanage in time? Was there within him that steely bit of soul that she'd always guessed at, that believed in the virtue of doing the right thing?

But then she understood that his face harboured only scorn, and he told her. "You? This is about *you* now? Moppet, this business gets me out of bloody Fountains Parish and into the Palace. Somehow, you got me a shot at a promotion, you worthless runt. Whatever the hell you're doing for the Archmagister, a whole load of his friends are pricking up their wizardly ears right now, and look who gets a pat on the head for keeping his eyes open."

And then the time for talk was done and he was hauling her back in the direction of the workshop, through all the buried ways beneath the palace, and when she demanded to know what had happened, he just yanked her arm harder, digging his fingers in to give her a bruise to remember him by.

~

She expected to be bundled into the workshop or its antechamber, that immaculate bedroom. Instead, she ended up somewhere else entirely, a small room set out as though two polite aristocrats were due to have tea there any moment, with a little lace-covered table and some chairs, a wall clock and a sideboard with some elegant porcelain figures that brought a stab of grief to Coppelia. Auntie Countless would have loved them.

The room was crowded beyond the dreams of decorum, though. The first her eyes lit on were a brace of magicians, one lord, one lady. Enough of a look passed between the man and Maulhands that Coppelia guessed this was the Catchpole's new patron. The wheels of her mind, that had been spinning all the way there, abruptly began to get some purchase on her situation.

Behind the pair of them, standing as though manacled to the wall despite the absence of actual chains, were some familiar faces. Shabby, Doctor Losef and Kernel Jointmaker, looking respectively surly, fearful and furious, but all of them at the mercy of their captors.

"Oh, she knows them," the mage-lord declared, smirking at Coppelia's look. "Do you, Catchpole?"

"The froggy one's an alchemist, pox doctor to half the Barrio. The big fellow was bully boy to the thief-lord who went up in smoke. The woman"—Maulhands gave Shabby a once-over—"no idea. Some thief."

"Fucker," Shabby spat at him, but Maulhands made a big show of not caring what gutter trash said to him.

"And no doubt in league with the little tinker brat

here," the mage-lord observed.

"You never said she was so young, Firmin," his companion said, sounding bored and resentful. "I thought she'd be something more like this specimen." She waved a hand near enough Shabby's face to get a finger bitten, though the thief prudently did no such thing.

"A villain, ma'am," Maulhands certified. "They grow them young in the Barrio, villainy from their very mother's teat."

Coppelia opened her mouth to point out the facts of her parents and their fate, and Lynx cuffed her almost absently, ramming her forwards until she almost broke a tooth against Jointmaker's chest. Reeling backwards, she caught a glimpse of something: movement about the big man's shoulders.

She made herself quiet, seeming very cowed even though her heart was racing. *They didn't come alone, the three thieves.* The grander implications of that were still rolling out in her head like a carpet, even as the captive rogues were hauled off by the mage-lord, and she herself by the Catchpole, all of them off to see the Archmagister. She saw this Firmin frown slightly, perhaps sensing a weakening of the bonds he'd set. He must have thought nothing of it, though, or guessed that the thieves themselves had some charms or tricks to aid escape, certainly not that a certain animate lump of wax had been diligently weakening the wards.

And then it *was* the bedchamber and the workshop, with Firmin striding self-importantly ahead, already smiling because he was about to score some points off his leader, and Coppelia could see that was meat and drink to the magi.

The golem wasn't sleeping, because sleep was something that living things did. It lay in the bed like a corpse at its own wake, though, sitting up smoothly as Firmin knocked and then entered.

"What is this?" its melodious voice demanded.

"Archmagister, there has been another incursion from the rabble," Firmin told him. "Your favourite pet has some new friends. I'm rather concerned that the freedom you've given her has allowed her to coordinate her larcenous efforts with the outside world, or how would they even have got in? It was only fortunate that Lucrece and myself happened to be in their way, or who knows what they might have made off with."

"Is that so?" There was nothing sharp or nasty in those musical tones, but Coppelia read them as such and knew she was right. The artificial man swung its metal legs over the side of the bed and stood smoothly, making the motions of shooting its cuffs even though the cuffs were rigid and one hand was still disassembled in the next room. *Something it saw people doing, and did not under-*

stand. Without a word, it walked into the workshop, forcing the entire cavalcade of others to follow.

It. Him. Must remember to call it "him." Her frame of reference slipped. It became the man Phenrir when it spoke with its lackeys or when she was hating it. When she worked on it, when she admitted its craftsmanship, it was a made thing, and somehow that was better.

She wasn't sure why it had retreated to the workshop at first, but once they'd followed, Phenrir turned on his steel heel in the centre of the room, and she felt the strings of power there, all the enchanted tools and machines that had been used to build him, that were attuned to the *made* far more than they would ever be to a mere *maker.* This was his place, where he was strongest, and he struck a casual pose there, in the centre of his web. Firmin must have felt it, too, but he was not taking the matter as seriously as he should. He was there to score points, but Coppelia knew that Phenrir was hunting very different game, because she'd put him on its trail.

"The Convocation is concerned," Firmin went on, utterly self-assured. "These rabble have dared our halls twice now." He gestured at the three thieves, Lynx and Belly Keach between them to haul them around, and their wrists still sorcerously bound. Coppelia was fighting not to stare, because there was definite movement within Jointmaker's sleeve. She had to keep her eyes anywhere but there, because Lucas Maulhands was at her own elbow, and he was watching her.

"And what have you done, our leader?" Firmin continued peevishly. "Stayed closeted up with this child-burglar, for reasons beyond our ken. You have it *working* for you, they say." He gestured towards the part-assembled hand on the workbench. "We lose confidence in you, Shorj."

"How fortunate we all were that you were on hand to apprehend them when they came again, Firmin," Phenrir said pleasantly. "How convenient, in fact. I have only one question for you, in that case."

Firmin's eyes narrowed slightly; presumably, he'd anticipated more asking than answering, if questions were to be handed out. Coppelia saw the woman, Lucrece, take one discreet step away from him, and liked her a little more for that.

"Where are the little people?" asked the Archmagister in his voice of glass and water.

"I . . ." Firmin blinked. "What?"

"Did you think I wouldn't notice?" the golem magus enquired, "that when they breached my sanctuary, they were guided by little men?"

"Little . . ." Firmin swallowed. ". . . men?" Coppelia was absolutely sure that his expression was blank puzzlement, but if you looked at it just so, and had a suspicious mind, it could be read as guilt.

"I know you and the others whisper behind my back, Firmin. Envy, that is what it is. I am Shorj Phenrir, the Archmagister of Loretz. And I always will be: eternal and ever-improving. This child has more skill in her fingers than any of you. She is more precious to me than you bloated bags of flesh with your intrigues and your sniggering. Don't think I haven't heard." And the terrible thing was, the voice remained on that wonderfully even keel, nothing in it giving rein to the venom of the words it chose. "She will make me better. She will make *me* better. And I will go on and on, and that is what you cannot abide."

"I . . ." Firmin blinked rapidly. "Little men?"

Lucrece was drawing away again, just one more soft step, and Coppelia was abruptly convinced she had a far better eye for magic than her companion.

"Your little men. Your metal magic men," Phenrir's golem pronounced perfectly. "You have been busy, Firmin, you and your fellows. You have been working to equal me. But you lack ambition. You started small. Still, small things are best suited to hidden deeds, I suppose. But did you really think I wouldn't notice?"

"Don't turn this back on me—" Firmin started, but the golem stamped, actually stamped like a petulant child, metal on stone ringing out like a bell-stroke.

"This is on you, Firmin. These rogues, their ingress which you manufactured, all to undermine me. I am the

Archmagister. I will brook no rivals. Live secure in your comfort and your indolence, by all means, but if you turn your eyes to the sun, they shall be burned from your skull!" And it made a grand gesture like an actor reaching for the painted silver paper of a theatre's fake sky, marred only by the lack of a hand within the sculpted cuff. And yet the socket there was not empty, not quite. Coppelia saw movement within, just for a moment. And so did Firmin, she was sure, for his eyes were huge in his head, like cracked eggs.

Because the last thing she needed right now was a free and frank exchange of information between them, she decided to drop the other shoe of her plan. "You're not the Archmagister, though."

Maulhands cuffed her almost absently and then found himself too close to the centre of attention because all eyes were on Coppelia. Phenrir's face was tilted, immaculate and expressionless, as though he listened only to birdsong from a further room.

"Shorj Phenrir worked well here," she whispered, and the golem nodded and said, "I did, I did," as though her previous words simply didn't exist in its memory.

Lucas shook her, but then the mage-woman, Lucrece, was there, driving him back with a look. "What is this?" she demanded quietly.

"He had the lore of Arcantel, probably. He made a

body to outlast the ages so he could cheat time. He was old, so old he'd countenance that kind of trick to give Death the slip," Coppelia said. She was almost whispering it, horrified at her own daring, incredulous that she hadn't been blasted to dust or bludgeoned like Auntie. "And he ran magic through that body, to Arcantel's design, I reckon. And then the body sat up, and he must have sat down and died, and it knew, somehow, what he'd been about. Maybe he'd told it what was in store for it when he made it. Maybe he gave it ears too soon. Maybe it even killed him when he gave it life, to prevent him playing cuckoo with its mind. But what sat up in this room was not Phenrir. It was a made thing, a thing of power but no more the Archmagister than a magic sword or dancing boots."

She heard a pin drop, in the silence that followed, or some other small metal part.

"What?" Firmin asked, and he hadn't taken it in, not really, because to do so would be to admit he'd been fooled all this time. Lucrece grasped it, though. Coppelia heard her whisper, "A made thing?" but most likely, she wasn't about to run out and trumpet the news all over the Siderea.

Most of all, she expected a curt denial from the golem, a wave of its absent hand to have her hauled off to a cell she'd never leave again, save for her own execution. She wasn't even sure it was true, just that the course of the magic within its body was simply that of the homunculi writ large, and where, then, was there room to encapsulate something as grand as the mind and being of a mage-lord? And of course, the hand she had made, which moved so inhumanly, yet Phenrir had not cared. It was her only shot, though, to sow more dissent between Phenrir and his underlings. But the false Archmagister just stood there, still as the statue it resembled, and when its voice came, it was halting.

"Is that how it happened?" it asked almost plaintively, and she had a belated rush of sympathy for it. It had killed Doublet and maimed Rosso, after all. It had cast itself as the grand villain, exploiter-in-chief of all Loretz. She'd never stopped to consider if it had been given a choice then, at the start, or how else it might have turned out in happier circumstances. She, of all people, should have thought about it.

"Archmagister . . . ?" Firmin asked, and the seeds were planted at last. His slack-jawed look had become something sharper and more suspicious. "Do you have anything to say?"

"I . . ." As though their positions were reversed, and one or the other of them had to be mumbling incomprehension at any given time.

Which was when the homunculi magicians within Jointmaker's sleeves finished breaking the magic that clamped his wrists together. Everyone else's attention was fixed on the golem, but Coppelia saw the moment, just a shift of the man's hands. She tensed, because surely Kernel would just explode into violence and focus everyone's ire on him and, by extension, his confederates including herself. He was an old rogue, though, as rogues went. His one move was to extend an elbow leftwards to dig into Shabby's ribs, an exaggerated mummery of a shared joke, save that Coppelia saw the rat-like flicker of movement as little bodies abandoned one ship for another.

"Oh, this is rare," Firmin said, and all doubt was gone from him. "Not the Archmagister but just some leftover *thing*, is it?" In his broad smile Coppelia could read a sunny future where he wore the fine robes and the big hat, or whatever made a mere mage-lord steeped in wealth and privilege into an Archmagister. "Well, we shall doubtless learn much from you in the laboratories. Catchpole, clap hands on the thing."

"Ah . . ." Lucas Maulhands had more-than-my-pay-grade written all over him. The golem was very still, though, head canted slightly downwards as though the revelation had robbed it of motion and speech. One hand still pincering Coppelia's arm, the Catchpole inched cautiously forward.

It seemed that insubordinate ambition grew like a

mushroom at all strata of the Siderea, though. Seeing his chief hesitate, Lynx Soriffo took one long stride and had the golem's metal sleeve under his fingers, already grinning at Firmin for approval.

"No!" The golem's bell-voice sounded cracked. When it ripped its arm from the Broadcap's grip, Coppelia saw a handful of tiny pieces—fastenings, washers—glint as they parted company from its joints. They were lost in the crack of Lynx's neck breaking as the golem backhanded him. All hell broke loose.

Firmin went for his magic immediately, so swift that Coppelia realised the man's superficiality had led her to seriously underestimate the threat he posed. His instinct was to shield himself first, attack later, though, dragging power from his rings and amulets to throw up a shimmering barrier between him and the golem rather than finishing the matter there and then.

"You can none of you live," decided the thing that wasn't Shorj Phenrir, and it sent a blast of power at Firmin just as it had half-incinerated Doublet. The human mage-lord was pushed backwards, soles leaving three-foot scuffs across the workshop floor, but his wall held, and his face twisted: not with fear but with outrage, that this *imposter* had inserted itself into the Convocation's select company. It was a *thing*, just as all lesser beings were *things* to the mage-lords. It had no right.

Shabby chose that moment to demonstrate that her hands were free by elbowing Belly Keach in the face, then lunging across Jointmaker to give Doctor Losef a shove. The baffled alchemist ended up on his back like a beetle, looking aggrieved until he realised he'd just inherited her cargo of homunculi. Shabby herself was trying to put space or workbenches between her fragile flesh and the magic that Firmin and the golem were throwing at each other.

Which left Lucas Maulhands. For a moment, he was frozen; she thought he'd go for the golem, or maybe just *go*. Instead, his vicelike grip on her arm doubled its pressure and he dragged his cudgel from his belt.

"You" was all he said. Meaning, in that language of oppressor and oppressed that they'd shared ever since she bit his hand and fled the orphanage, that it was all her fault, all of it. And, like so many of his suspicions about her, it was true.

"Yes," she agreed, and tried to knee him in the maritals, on the basis that any damage there was saving the women of Loretz future disappointment. Maulhands was an old hand at street fighting, though, taking the blow on the outside of his thigh and then just shaking her, a whipcrack of motion passing from his arm through her entire body, so that she bit her tongue and lost track of what she was about for a moment, long enough for him to slam her down onto a bench, spilling gold shavings and callipers and a fountain of brass screws onto the floor. The cudgel came up with the clear aim of having her brains join them.

She saw a flicker of motion reflected in the club's polished head. Maulhands must have had more of an eye out, because he was already turning to catch Jointmaker's charge and throw the man past him. Kernel was slightly on fire, and Coppelia realised the enforcer had just lunged past the magi, too heedless or ignorant to care about the power there. He hooked the Catchpole's collar as his own balance was swiped from him, so that the pair of them ended up on the ground, fighting furiously to get on top. Maulhands gave Kernel a glancing blow across the temple with his club, but the enforcer took it in order to secure the hilt of Lucas's knife. The Catchpole got one hand on his wrist, preventing him from drawing it out, but Jointmaker had done a similar service with Maulhand's cudgel arm, leaving the pair of them grunting and straining, rolling back and forth and trying to get a knee or a forehead somewhere useful to break the stalemate.

Which left Coppelia.

She looked around frantically. Shabby was on the far side of the room, in a corner with Belly Keach on one side and far too much magic on the other to get out of the man's reach. Behind the big Broadcap, though, Doctor

Losef was on his feet and fumbling for his bandolier. That little skirmish was hopefully going to resolve itself, therefore, but it didn't help Jointmaker, and Maulhands was living up to his name now. The Catchpole was steadily bending his enemy back against the floor, getting a knee up to pin Kernel's chest down.

Coppelia's fingers touched something cool and slender; they knew it for what it was from long familiarity, and she had no time to find something better.

She went for Maulhands with it, bringing the point down towards his head like a mummer's dagger. Of course, the Catchpole saw her coming. He was already swaying back to spoil her aim, shifting his weight so that instead of driving her makeshift weapon into his eye, she instead splintered it against his chest. A paintbrush, no more than that, and one of the slender ones for delicate work. The shock was enough, though; just for one moment, he thought she'd stabbed him. Kernel Jointmaker took that moment and, like a painter drawing an image from bare canvas, made it a reality, yanking the knife out from Lucas's momentarily nerveless fingers and then ramming the blade home into the man's armpit, unseaming his robe and then the rest of him.

There was a horrible shrieking going on. Possibly, it had been going on for a few seconds already, but Coppelia noticed it only now. It was Firmin, and at first she thought it was because he was losing. His face admitted nothing of it, though, and he was holding his ground against the golem's assault. The screaming, the screwed-up spoiled-child expression, was nothing more than his former outrage given vent. He was howling at this made thing, this imposter, to give up and know its place. Even as his shields cracked, even as his exhausted rings tarnished and his amulets blackened, it was the sheer *affront* that moved him. He screamed at Lucrece to join him, but the woman was over in the corner by Shabby, the pair of them keeping well clear. The mage-lady's expression was naked in her desire to see *something* happen to Firmin, and if that something was being blasted apart by a golem, she'd take it.

That was not what happened, though. Coppelia found she'd almost been waiting for it. Even as he roared his fury and sent a faintly leonine wave of fire to pounce upon the false Phenrir, a gleaming little shape appeared on Firmin's shoulder. And, because he was who he was, Arc spent a valuable second brandishing his tiny blade at the world, the hero conquering giants in a tattered gown.

"Ah!" The golem actually staggered, seeing him there, and Firmin, ignorant, simply used the moment to push further, the force of his magic ramming the metal form back across a bench. His cry of victory came out in two pieces because Arc cut his throat right in the middle of it, no respecter of drama when it was someone else's limelight.

The room was very quiet after that. Belly Keach was on the ground, smiling weirdly as the result of whatever Doctor Losef had stuck him with. The alchemist, Shabby and Lucrece were clumped together for mutual protection. Kernel was sitting down by Maulhands's cooling corpse.

Firmin finally knelt before his Archmagister, albeit mostly posthumously. His lips flapped a bit, unable to give voice to his final thoughts on the matter. Then he fell sideways, waifs and strays of magic discharging from his fingers, his clothes and jewellery.

With a screech of metal, the golem righted itself. Coppelia heard a hundred little parts go rattling and tinkling down its hollow insides. For a moment, it just passed its benevolent expression across them all. Much of its enamel and painting was gone, but what was revealed was polished to a shine by the blast of Firmin's magic. Light sprang from it, painful to look at in its beauty.

"You can none of you live," it repeated calmly. "I am the Archmagister. I will kill the truths in you. Nobody will ever know." Its gaze swung to Coppelia, the architect of its problems, and it extended a hand to her as though about to twirl her off across a ballroom. Power limned every joint of those fingers she had designed and redesigned. It stepped towards her; it was going to obliter-ate her with her own work.

With a musical clang, its other arm came off at the elbow, the handless sleeve section bounding across the floor like an eager dog.

"I . . ." said the golem, and its remaining thumb came away, and then the rest of the hand even as it reached for her, the pieces of her artifice pattering like rain. "How . . . ?" And she said nothing, wanting it to believe at the end that she had somehow engineered this betrayal, the seeds of it placed invisibly within her workmanship. It would never know otherwise. It would not know, when that entire arm parted company from its shoulder, that Tef would be crouching in the hole, busily dismantling another section.

One leg collapsed, joints separating out into individ-ual pieces. The golem crashed to a knee, to its front. It was making sounds, but they weren't words anymore. Then its head fell off and another homunculus sprang from the stump of its neck, brandishing a tiny spear in one hand and a screwdriver (the smallest size for the finest work, naturally) in the other.

"Fuck," said Kernel Jointmaker, and then "Fuck!" be-cause he'd seen Lucrece and she had not squandered any of her magic and had a throat still entirely unslit. For a moment, Coppelia thought that the fighting was about to come back for another race around the room, but then the woman shuddered and shook her head.

"Just go," she told them. "Take things, if you have to, but get out of the Siderea. I'll say it was all Firmin. Now he's dead, nobody will remember they were friends of his." Which probably meant that Belly Keach wouldn't be waking up, but Coppelia reckoned that was what you got for dealing with magicians. Why Lucrece wasn't just striking them all dead was another matter, but then the woman eyed Shabby and said, "You, though. You can come back, if you want." And a wink, just like those cheap romances even a Moppet knew about. From Shabby's expression, Coppelia reckoned the thief just might, at that.

13.

THE HAND WAS PERFECT. A bad artisan blamed her tools, Coppelia knew, and she thanked hers. They were, after all, quite literally the best money could ever have bought—and this was Loretz, where money bought magic and magic bought money in an ever-increasing spiral, so long as you already had more of both than you could ever need. And of course, the doubly late Shorj Phenrir would have made sure his personal workshop was stocked with the best so that his slave artisans could provide him with the most elegant new body for his intended everlasting existence.

It was not in seeing the golem come apart that Coppelia had felt her long-lost parents avenged; it was in taking these tools for herself, bringing them to her shoddy little studio in the Barrio.

Up on the Siderea, everything was calm, and nobody was even mentioning the extinction of the Archmagister. Nobody was naming a new one, either, and Shabby brought regular updates on the vicious political knife-fighting between various members of the

Convocation seeking to take that coveted comfy seat. Several of the mage-lords had elected to leave the city to tour sites of historical interest, apparently, and sometimes that boiled down to exile, and sometimes it was just a convenient way of saying that assassin-magic had overcome protection-magic. In the meantime, the Barrioni were steadily expanding their own hold on the city, expanding across the river and ensuring the Broadcaps trod lightly and looked away when necessary. And Coppelia knew on an intellectual level that this was no great victory for justice—possibly quite the reverse—but that didn't stop her vicariously exalting when Shabby and her fellows told the stories of what they'd got away with.

When the homunculi came down to her later, she showed them her work: four new bodies of wood, and one trial piece in metal, still not her favourite material. She had plans to wrangle some apprenticeships with other artisans, though: candle-makers, tailors, bone-workers. She had a demanding and varied clientele, after all. Or perhaps she would take on workers from the host of half-mage professionals drawn to Loretz. She was building her own little empire.

Shallis looked over the vessels, crinkling as she bent to examine the fine work. The Folded One, as the homunculi called her, still sent skitters of unease through Coppelia: that face of lines and creases looking like something mummified, that scratchy little voice so sharp with disapproval. Shallis could find nothing to disapprove of this time, though, and at last she nodded, and Lief and the others carried the little mannikins off up to the attic. All save Arc and Tef, who were on other business.

"We're going out with Shabby tonight. Big job, rich house," Arc declared. He had replaced his gown with a finer one, stolen from some merchant's daughter's favourite doll. The bright colours and elaborate cut made him into a barbaric warlord from an ancient age. His daughter was even finer, though. *Daughter*, despite Auntie's music-box dancer being made to look male, because the homunculi had some residual concept of gender from their long-ago creator, but to them it was just a thing that differentiated parent from child, so that their generations flipped one to the other without any grander meaning than that.

"Be careful," Coppelia warned them. Arc struck an indignant pose and even Tef waved off the warning.

"That magician friend of hers has cleared the way for us," she called up, meaning their target was probably some enemy of Lucrece's she was setting Shabby on. Or alternatively that Shabby was setting Lucrece on the richest plums in the Siderea. Coppelia didn't feel she could enquire as to the full details of the pair's new relationship.

She had thought Shabby might make herself the new thief-lord in the parish, but instead one of the neighbouring magnates had just expanded to take over the Iron End's estates. On the surface, it all looked just like before, even down to Kernel Jointmaker at the new lord's right hand. Except Coppelia knew that there had been some spectacular finagling accompanying the new Barrion's coronation. The man had taken his throne only after a few clandestine agreements, motivated by discovering a razor blade at his neck one morning, as he slept in his impregnable sanctum behind all his traps and guards and magical wards. He would profit well in his new power and parish, he understood, but his hand would rest lightly there, and he would have some new lieutenants, including a master-thief, an alchemist and a girl who these days was becoming a puppeteer in more ways than one.

~

Above, in the attic, Shallis and the others laid out the new bodies in the Blue Lantern Chamber, which had been expanded to fit their new wealth and was already crackling with power looking for a home. Much of their takings had been exported by raven to the other colonies, a tiny countercurrent to the great acquisitive greed of the mage-lords in drawing all magic in to Loretz. They had kept plenty for themselves, though, enough for all the bodies the Moppet could turn out for them. Rings they had, and monocles, hatpins, brooches and crystals, geartrains, lamps, lost toys and overlooked keepsakes. And at the heart of it, the pillar against which all this piecemeal hoard was shored, a metal head regarded all the clutter and the bustle of new life with fixed, beatific features.

About the Author

Author photograph © Kate Eshelby

ADRIAN TCHAIKOVSKY is the author of the acclaimed Shadows of the Apt fantasy series and the epic science fiction blockbuster *Children of Time*. He has won the Arthur C. Clarke Award and the British Fantasy Award, and he has been nominated for the David Gemmell Legend Award. In civilian life he is a lawyer, gamer, and amateur entomologist.

TOR·COM

Science fiction. Fantasy. The universe.

And related subjects.

*

More than just a publisher's website, *Tor.com*
is a venue for **original fiction, comics,** and
discussion of the entire field of SF and fantasy,
in all media and from all sources. Visit our site
today—and join the conversation yourself.